the butterfly heart

Paula Leyden was born in Kenya and spent her childhood in Zambia. As a teenager she moved with her family to South Africa, where she soon became involved in the struggle to end Apartheid. Since 2003 she has lived on a farm in Kilkenny, Ireland, with her partner and five children, where she breeds horses and writes. *The Butterfly Heart* is Paula's first novel.

Paula Leyden

WALKER
BOOKS

This is a work of fiction. Names, characters, places and incidents
are either the product of the author's imagination or, if real, are used
fictitiously. All statements, activities, stunts, descriptions, information
and material of any other kind contained herein are included for
entertainment purposes only and should not be relied on for
accuracy or replicated, as they may result in injury.

First published 2011 by Walker Books Ltd
87 Vauxhall Walk, London SE11 5HJ

2 4 6 8 10 9 7 5 3

Text © 2011 Paula Leyden

This book has been typeset in Bembo and Kosmik Bold

Printed and bound in Great Britain by Clays Ltd, St Ives plc

British Library Cataloguing in Publication Data:
a catalogue record for this book is
available from the British Library

ISBN 978-1-4063-2792-2

www.walker.co.uk

For Tom, Amy, Christie, Kate,
Aisling and Maurice

Bul-Boo

My friend Winifred didn't put her hand up today. Not once. She hardly put her *head* up. I kept looking at her sideways, waiting. But nothing. When the bell rang, she slipped out of the classroom as if she had never been there. Like a shadow. I stayed sitting for a while, wondering. Maybe she was having a quiet day. Surely everyone has those? Or maybe she didn't know any answers. No. Not likely.

I felt Madillo patting me on the head, my daily signal that it was time to pack my bag to go home. There is nothing shadow-like or silent about my twin sister, Madillo. I wonder how much Mum and Dad knew about armadillos when they named her after one. Not very much, I think, because apart from the odd grunt they are peaceful creatures.

"Hey, Bul-Boo, I'm not waiting more than twenty-three seconds for you today … and two of those have gone already. Now seven… You're out of time. I'm leaving…"

She danced towards the door, holding her bag on her head.

I followed her. I don't really like walking home on my own. If Madillo is with me then no one notices me, even though we look the same. She makes more noise than I do. This afternoon she decided to count the number of steps she took … in Japanese. In our bedroom, on the ceiling above her bed, she has stuck up a chart with the numbers from one to 999,999 in Japanese. When the light is out she shines her torch onto them and counts out loud. That way, she says, they grow in her head during the night – and it is working. But she thinks one million is unlucky, so she has not learnt how to say that.

Winifred and I have been sitting next to each other in class for two years now. Our teacher, Sister Leonisa, doesn't like change, and all the time we've been in her class no one has ever moved seats. She kept a dead pot plant on the windowsill for a whole term once because she didn't want to move it, so when you sit next to someone you know that will be it. I think if you died in your seat she probably wouldn't move you. But I suppose your parents would when they heard.

Winifred is the same age as me, except I was born in the wet season and her birthday is in the dry season. She is short and neat and the tidiest (and cleverest) person in our class. On her side of the desk there is hardly anything to be seen, a fact that Sister always points out to me. As if I couldn't see it for myself.

"Look, Bul-Boo," she says, "can you see any pencil shavings on Winifred's side of the desk? Any ugly bits of paper? Any pens leaking all over the place? Anything at all except the things that have to be there, the things that have no option?"

"No, Sister," I always reply.

If I was Madillo, I might say, "Yes, Sister, because I see all … even that which isn't there," and see what she'd say to that. But I'm not, so I won't. However, I do wonder why she keeps asking me when it clearly makes no difference. And Winifred doesn't mind, even when I spill over onto her side. She tells me that at home there is no room to be messy. I've never thought about it like that, but it makes sense: if you're messy in a small space then you can't move.

I always think that Winifred doesn't mind about anything: she never gets cross or mad like Madillo does.

But maybe I'm wrong. She was minding about something today.

We normally walk halfway home with her, then we go left and she goes right – and it takes us ages because we always have so much to talk about. Winifred is almost as good at telling stories as Ifwafwa is, and sometimes (if we can stop Madillo counting) she tells us some on the way home. The only time we are ever in a hurry is when the rain comes. None of us mind the rain but we hate lightning. Today Winifred didn't tell a story; she didn't even laugh when Madillo fell down (as she does most days), she just carried on walking with her head down. I wondered if I'd said something to upset her but I didn't want to ask, her face was so closed.

We took much longer than usual to get home after we had split from Winifred, because Madillo reached 362 steps and then made a mistake. Even though I told her where she had got to, she didn't believe me and had to start again. When it comes to numbers, the only person she trusts is herself.

As it turned out, it was lucky she did go back because we met Ifwafwa, the Snake Man – and if we'd gone straight home we might have missed him. He promised to come by tomorrow, as he has a new story.

Ifwafwa

Ifwafwa. Yes, that's what they call me. The Puff Adder. Slow and heavy, but fast to strike. The little one, Bul-Boo, she told me about that name. It's a nickname, she said, because you catch all the snakes and because your bicycle makes that noise, *fwa-fwa-fwa*. Then she asked me, "Why do you put those little bits of orange plastic on your wheel spokes, Mr Snake Man?" She's full of respect, a serious child. She wants to know everything. I think that life will be kind to her.

I told her that the plastic is to warn the snakes that I'm coming and that they should pack their bags and say their goodbyes because they'll be moving out. She liked that. She has a laugh that is so loud it is hard to believe it comes out of such a small child.

I put the plastic there because I like the sound it makes. It keeps me awake when I ride my bicycle. When the sun is hot and I'm travelling a long straight road, it is easy for me to fall asleep. Especially if I'm hungry for food. But not any more. The *fwa-fwa-fwa* makes me think about different things. When I think, I stay awake.

Today I thought about Nsanguni, the snake of all snakes. She is so long that if you stood at her head you could not see her tail. She is not a snake for catching.

Nsanguni is from the water. Her home is the river. It is always wise to keep your distance from her. It is the shadow she wants: your shadow. At night time you are safe because your shadow is missing, but when the sun shines and your shadow lies on the ground, help-less, Nsanguni takes it. Swallows it whole. As it travels down her long body, it takes you with it and you follow because you are nobody without your shadow. Then you are gone. Dead. Lost in her body.

One day, maybe, she'll get tired and full and spit all the shadows out onto the riverbank. There will be much rejoicing when that day comes.

Bul-Boo

Winifred was late today. It was the first time she has been late, ever. We could be in the middle of the biggest thunderstorm and Winifred will arrive at school on time, with plastic bags tied carefully around her shoes so they don't get muddy. Where her house is, there is a long muddy road she has to walk down before she reaches the tar road, but her shoes are always clean.

Today was a normal sunny day but she arrived at half past eight – half an hour late. She didn't even say anything to Sister, she just crept in the same way she crept out yesterday. So quietly I am not even sure if Sister noticed. Maybe Winifred knew beforehand that we were going to get the Tapeworm Speech. She was lucky she missed it, especially first thing in the morning before anyone had even had time to digest their breakfast. I think Winifred would have been worried by it, too – even more than we were – because she seems to be getting thinner and thinner, and that's one of the signs of having a tapeworm.

Sister was so excited at the thought of giving us this speech that she forgot to say morning prayers. She just stood up, clapped her hands and asked, "Who has heard about the tapeworm?" We all put our hands up then, because who hasn't?

"Good. Now, who knows how to entice a tapeworm out of your body?"

She always uses words like "entice". She once said to us that if there is an exciting word available, why choose a boring one. I suppose that makes sense.

No one answered this time.

"So I am going to tell you. Me, Sister Leonisa, a lion among nuns."

I looked across the room at Madillo, who I just knew would be grinning all over her face. Any distraction from work or morning prayers is her favourite thing. With Sister Leonisa we often have distractions, but they aren't always good, so I was feeling a bit nervous.

"When a tapeworm makes its entrance into your

body, it is nothing more than a small egg. But quickly it transforms itself into a long, ribbony worm with an insatiable appetite. It eats all the time, without stopping. It is the glutton of the worm world."

Sister drew a long, ribbony tapeworm on the board in a few quick strokes, then added the largest mouth I have ever seen. She even put teeth in it. Sharp, pointy teeth.

"Every time you put food into your mouth, all you are doing is feeding the worm. It sits there with its own mouth open, waiting for the food to arrive."

Madillo had stopped smiling now and I could feel this long tapeworm inside me. I was sure it was listening to every word Sister was saying and just waiting for breaktime, when it could begin eating again.

"So how do we stop this monstrous creature from eating all our food?"

There was silence. Fred, our next-door neighbour (who I will tell you about) was bent over his desk, not even looking at Sister. He was clutching his stomach.

"I'll tell you," she said. "You starve it. Deprive it of food. Don't give it anything, not a morsel, for three days. By that time it will be your slave. It will do anything for you. After the three days are up, pour a little milk into a saucer and go and sit somewhere comfortable. Open your mouth and hold the saucer in front of you like this." She held the chalkboard rubber in front of her wide-open mouth.

"You will feel a sudden movement in your stomach: it is your worm realizing there is food near by. It is sitting up now, its mouth open and waiting. But nothing happens. It has become mad with hunger, so it leaves its comfortable home and sets off to look for the food. It creeps up from your stomach into your throat and pops its head out of your mouth."

All our mouths were wide open. Not a word from anyone.

"As it sees the milk, it bends down and starts lapping it up with its tongue. When you hear the first little laps, you must reach up with your other hand, grab its head and start pulling as fast as you can. Do not close your mouths now, children, or you will bite it in half and it'll wriggle right back inside you and start growing another head. Pull and pull until you reach its tail." She paused for breath as she showed us how to do this. "It could be three metres long, depending on how well you have been feeding it, so this part can take a long time. When it is out, stamp on it over and over again till you are sure it's dead. And that, girls and boys, is that. One dead tapeworm and one happy and healthy child."

I think Sister Leonisa is a bit mad. I am one hundred per cent sure that worms don't have tongues or teeth, and I do not think they are able to smell. At least Sister didn't draw a nose on her worm. I must tell Mum and Dad this story. Or maybe I won't. They like coming into school to have their say and they'd certainly have something to say about this.

Anyway, it was just as Sister Leonisa was finishing her speech that Winifred arrived. Sister probably didn't notice her because she was too busy stamping her imaginary tapeworm to death.

Ifwafwa

I knew home once, when I was young. I knew my mother. She was tall and her back was straight. She could look into the sun without blinking her eyes, and pass her hand slowly through flames without feeling pain. People said that she had inherited magic ways from my grandmother; that she was a *muloshi*, a witch. She could do things other people couldn't. Some of the people in our village were scared of her, but others came to her for help. She never lied to them. If she could help, and if the helping was for good, then she would. If there was nothing she could do, she would tell them, "No, this is not for me. This is a sadness I cannot change. I am not strong enough for that." Those people would leave with their heads hanging, and I think it was they who started the talk against her.

For me, she was just my mother. She was my home. The path back from school was always long and hot, but when I reached the tree on the corner I knew I was close. Always at that tree the hot tasty smell of porridge, the *nshima*, would float towards me on the wind and I would run and leave the dust behind me. On Fridays sometimes she would cook kapenta fish, silvery and salty. In the rainy season there would be mangoes for me, picked from the tree at the back and brought inside to cool.

But it was not my mother who taught me how to talk to the snakes, it was my grandmother. She had lived with us ever since I was born and she told me that she could see I had a gift, a gift that was good. *Her* grandmother had had the same gift and she had been quiet and slow, like me. She told me how her grandmother would sit under the shade of a tree and sing. If there were snakes near by, they would come to her. She would sit still, her small thin legs stretched out in front of her, and the snakes would draw closer. Some would come and rest against her and others on her. She never moved. When she stopped singing, they would leave.

I did not know her, but sometimes she is here with me. Sometimes I hear her singing voice. It says things to me. My grandmother would have been happy to know that the old lady, her own grandmother, visits me. Maybe they are together now. Maybe they are both watching over my mother, who died before she was ready.

Bul-Boo

We waited at the gate when we got home so that we would be there when Ifwafwa arrived. He had promised to come, and he never breaks his promises and never lies. Which, if you think about it, is an unusual thing to be able to say about someone. I know there is a difference between small, necessary lies to make other people happy and really large lies that are – well, just big and not very good. But Ifwafwa doesn't even tell the small ones. Or if he does, I don't notice.

It was Fred's great-granny who first told us about him. Fred says that she is a very famous witch and that even Alice Lenshina was scared of her. That is something to brag about. Alice Lenshina started this kind of a church called Lumpa, meaning "better than all the others" in Bemba, which is one of the languages I speak. (I say Bemba, although I am supposed to say Chibemba because that is the proper name – but Dad says it's OK to use the shortened version.) So Alice Lenshina's mission was to rid Zambia of sorcery and witchcraft, and if she – with her army of something like 100,000 followers – was scared of Fred's great-granny, then Fred is right, she must be famous. And very scary. Alice is long dead now, but Fred's great-granny is still alive. She is the oldest person I have ever seen. You cannot even see her eyes any more because of the wrinkles.

A couple of years ago she told us that if we ever had problems with snakes, we should look out for a kind man on a big black bicycle. We would know him by the sound he makes as he rides around, she said, because he has tied little bits of orange plastic onto the spokes of his wheels, so you can hear him coming. You wouldn't imagine you could tell that someone was kind just by looking at them on their bicycle, but with Ifwafwa she was right. We did find him, and since that day he has been our friend.

When Ifwafwa arrived he was carrying his bag, and we could see from the bumps that there were snakes inside.

Madillo is always excited if Ifwafwa has snakes with

him because he lets her stroke them. I have only tried that once. They do feel soft and dry, not slimy, but I still don't like the feeling of their muscles moving under their skin. I told Ifwafwa once that that's what people call him, the Puff Adder, but he didn't mind. For him, it's not an insult to be called a snake name, because he loves them.

He sat down on the grass and we sat down next to him, me the furthest away from the snake bag, and he began.

"This is the story of the Bangweulu Swamps, the place where the water and the sky meet and become one, the place where the lechwe live: the red deer with the legs that can leap in the water. It is not near my home, it is in the place of the Kaonde people."

When the Snake Man tells us a story, he tells it in a very quiet voice so it is hard for us to hear him. He is clever like that; he makes us listen. Sister Leonisa does the opposite, shouting and waving her arms around, some-times even jumping up and down. With her we have no option but to listen, but with Ifwafwa we want to.

"A long time ago a small child, only a little bigger than you," he said, nodding his head towards me, "was playing down by the river. She was with her mother, who was drawing water. A black shadow fell across them and the mother looked up into the sky, as they had been waiting for the rains for many months. Then she heard her small daughter scream and turned around.

"The Kongamato, the one they all dreaded meeting, was swooping down out of the sky towards the little girl. Its long beak was wide open and the mother could see its teeth. Its huge wings blocked the sun. It was almost upon them when the mother reached up and grabbed hold of its tail. She held on tight – she did not want her little girl taken from her – but the Kongamato was too strong for her and grabbed the child and flew up into the sky. The mother managed to keep her grip and the creature flew away silently, carrying them both as if they weighed no more than a flake of ash."

The Snake Man looked at Madillo and me. "Do you know of the Kongamato? The overwhelmer of boats?"

We shook our heads, hardly daring to breathe.

"It is a bird without feathers. A lizard with wings. A creature like no other, with a beak and teeth. It flies slowly and has lived on this earth since time began. Its skin is like a snake's, soft and smooth. No one knows where it goes to rest, but it always flies around the Bangweulu Swamps. It causes floods by stopping the river and there is no boat in this world that can resist it; no person either, for to look into its eyes is death. The Kaonde people make a potion to protect themselves against it, only this poor mother and her child had forgotten to use it. No one ever saw them again. The Kongamato returned alone."

Ifwafwa sat back on the grass in silence. Then he opened the top of his sack slightly to check that his snakes were still well. He smiled then closed it again. That's the downside of him not telling lies: he doesn't have many stories with happy endings.

"Is it real?" Madillo asked.

He looked at her. "Do you think it is, my dear? People have seen it many times. They all speak of the same thing: of the wings that are wider than I am tall, of the beak that is longer than the tail. It is real when you have seen it, yes. I hope you never will."

Madillo shivered but did not look worried. She likes getting scared. These kinds of things fly out of her head as quickly as they arrive, but they stay in mine. I will have to try and think very hard about something else, otherwise the Kongamato will visit me tonight in my dreams.

Ifwafwa

It is a long life when you are one. One on your own.
That is why I tell stories. When I tell stories, my head is
filled with other people who talk to me and know me.
When I tell stories, my mother and grandmother come
back to me. My grandmother scolds me and sends me
off to look for eggs. I hear my mother laughing. People
whose names have gone from my head appear again
and I can look into their faces and know them. I like it
when my head is busy like that.

When I was smaller than Bul-Boo and her sister, I
started listening to people when they couldn't see me.
I cannot explain why. Crouching low, I sat outside their
windows and heard the things they said. Bad things and

good things. But it all stopped the day Winston found me and beat me till I couldn't walk.

He was much bigger than me, a man, and he took a stick to me and beat me as I was lying on the ground, shouting so loudly that everyone came to look. He said he would beat the devil out of me, the witch's heathen child. It was my grandmother who stopped him. He was afraid of her. She ran out of our house on her thin legs and I heard her voice: "Winston." Nothing else. Not loud, no shouting. Just that. He stopped and looked around, I think to make sure who was speaking. When he saw her, he moved away from me. He looked scared.

I did not get up; I lay there absolutely still. If I moved, I thought it would start again. I did not even open my eyes or my ears. Then my grandmother came over to me and knelt down in the dust. She put her head next to mine. "Come, little one. You are all right now." She helped me home and for three days and nights she looked after me, taking away the pain. Winston never touched me again.

But he waited a long time, and then he touched her.

Bul-Boo

Dad went up north today, so he wasn't home for supper, and I wonder if Mum deliberately chooses these times to give us lectures. This one started at supper because Madillo made a speech about being older than me and how that meant she should always get her food first. She did come out first – that bit is true – but identical twins are really only two people by accident. One egg splits and two embryos grow instead of one. So technically she is not older.

Whenever Mum gets an opportunity to tell us how lucky we are, she takes it. So she leapt in. "Madillo, instead of wanting to be first in the queue, you should be grateful for your mere existence."

That silenced both of us. I could have expected the usual "millions of children wouldn't mind *when* they got food as long as they got something…" But not this.

"If you were horses…" Mum went on. "Well, if *I* was a horse that had fallen pregnant with twins, the vet would be called and one of the eggs would be pinched to death. One of *you*."

"Pinched to death? I've never heard of that." I didn't like the way this conversation was going.

"Yes. Pinched. So it withers away. And the mare – *me*, in this case – is left with only one foal. One of *you*, in other words."

"Well, that'd only be if you were a tame horse," Madillo said. "If you were wild, there'd be no vet to call and then both of us would be born. Then I might demand to get food first."

"Or you'd both die, taking me along with you. And, on the subject of existence, what if one of you had disappeared? It's a phenomenon, you know: the Phenomenon of the Disappearing Twin." Mum announces things like that as if they are just daily occurrences, twins disappearing all over the place, never to be seen again.

"In humans or horses?" I said.

"I'm talking humans here, Bul-Boo," she said. "Twins can show up on a scan and then, by the time of the next scan, one of them has disappeared. There is evidence to suggest that it disappears into the other twin. If that had happened in your case, either one of you could have ended up with a tiny pre-human embedded somewhere in your body."

Mum sat back and started eating again, as if she had just had a perfectly normal conversation. I could have lived my whole life quite happily without knowing any of these facts.

"Is there a Phenomenon of the Disappearing Triplet?" Madillo asked.

"There is."

"I have always had a feeling there was someone else in my life… I wonder where she's embedded? Maybe in my shoulder. I think I'll call her Mary."

For pretty obvious reasons both Madillo and I like simple names: Mary, Anna, Emily – they all sound good to us. If we had names like that, no one would ever ask us, "Now, dear, how do you spell that?"

"What makes you think she's in your shoulder and not mine?" I asked.

"I feel her presence, a small tingling presence." This was all said in perfect Madillo style, whispery with a "no further discussion" kind of sound to it.

"Madillo, don't talk nonsense," Mum said, as if it hadn't been her who had planted the idea in the first place.

This got me thinking about being a twin. It is almost all good being a twin, mainly because I always have someone to talk to. There are a few downsides, like being referred to as "the twins", as if that explains everything. (We do have names; we are not, as Dr Seuss might have had us, Twin One and Twin Two; we are, in fact, very different from each other.) But I am glad Madillo is my twin, even though I didn't have much choice about it. And I am glad that Mum and Dad are not horses, because knowing my luck I would have been the one to have been pinched.

I decided that after supper I would ask Madillo about Winifred, to see whether she had noticed her strange behaviour too. So when we had done the washing-up and were left in the kitchen – that's where we do our homework – I asked if she had noticed anything strange about Winifred recently. Madillo leant forward. "Strange? What kind of strange?" she said.

"Well, she doesn't put her hand up any more, she's been late for school … and I think she's getting thinner. I can see it in her face."

Madillo closed her eyes briefly. "Probably spirit possession. What else could it be, with those symptoms? That must be it. Come to think of it, her eyes have been looking a bit odd recently…"

All this from someone who had not noticed

anything until I pointed it out! Madillo sat back, waiting for me to agree with her.

Generally, agreeing is the best thing to do with Madillo. The easy route would have been to nod and say something like "Mmm, it could be… You never know", as if spirit possession was one of a normal range of possibilities. I do not usually take the easy route. So I raised my left eyebrow and said, "Really?" to give her the opportunity to expand. She needed no second invitation.

"Well, three things have happened, according to you, in the space of a week: she's stopped putting up her hand, she was late and she's getting thinner. Have you noticed what she actually does when Sister asks a question?"

"She just sits there with her head down," I answered.

"I think if you looked a little closer, you might see a silent struggle going on between her and her spirit occupier. You'd probably see her trying to put her hand up but not being able to. I think her spirit is evil…"

Madillo was in full swing now.

"That's rubbish and you know it," I said, knowing I would be ignored.

"And her face getting thinner? You have some other explanation for that, Bul-Boo?"

"Weight loss? Tapeworm? Worry?" I said. "Three million reasons that would be better than yours."

She shook her head and said solemnly, "No, I think the spirit is eating away at her."

It seemed like a good time to end the conversation. Evil spirits aren't really my thing, and no matter what I said, nothing would change my sister's mind anyway.

Bul-Boo

I didn't think about the Kongamato much last night because my head was too full of Winifred. I was remembering the time Madillo and I became friends with her.

It was after we discovered that she also knew the Snake Man, Ifwafwa. One day in class we were doing English and Sister asked us to make up a story about trees. I couldn't think of anything but Madillo was the first to volunteer. It's quite something to watch Madillo tell a story because she's pretty dramatic about it.

She went and stood at the front of the class, even though she could have stayed at her desk. And then she started.

"This is my story of the Kondanamwali – the tree

that eats maidens. It is the biggest baobab tree known to humans, and it stands proudly in the Kafue National Park. Once upon a time four beautiful girls lived in the shade of this tree, and lo and behold, it fell in love with them."

You can see what I mean about the drama. She loves phrases like "lo and behold", and her tale was accompanied by hand-waving and crouching and whispering. Pretty impressive, I have to admit – you wouldn't catch me doing that for anything.

Madillo looked around the class. "Yes, it fell in love with all four of them at the same time. Smitten with a terrible love. When they grew up, the four young maidens decided one night to leave the tree and go off in search of husbands. The tree heard them planning this; it heard their giggles and became wildly jealous. The night before they planned to leave, there was a raging thunderstorm. No one had ever seen or heard anything like it. The lightning flashed and darted and the thunder terrified the young maidens. They cowered by the trunk of the giant tree.

"This suited the tree very well and it opened up its great trunk and swallowed them. They had no idea where they were. All they knew was that suddenly they were dry, they couldn't hear the thunder and it was dark all about them. They clung to one another in terror as they slowly realized that they were inside the tree. There was no escape.

"And there they have been ever since. On stormy nights you can hear them crying inside the tree – people who live there are afraid to go near it. That is one of the reasons why you should never seek shelter under a tree when there is lightning." Madillo paused and looked at Winifred, who was sitting next to me, right at the front of the classroom. "Would you go near it, Winifred?"

Winifred was smiling. "No, Madillo. Why would I? I don't want to be swallowed by a tree."

Madillo turned back to the class, clapped her hands and bowed. "So, Sister, that is my story of a tree."

Sister Leonisa isn't usually free with praise, but she did say a grudging well done to Madillo. At that point Winifred – who I did not know very well yet – whispered in my ear, "I know that story; the Snake Man told it to me."

So that was why she had been smiling: she'd known it wasn't Madillo's story. At breaktime I told this to Madillo, who blushed a little but then ran off to talk to Winifred.

When the Snake Man told us that story, I remember asking him why he didn't go and get the maidens out, because – as far as I can see – he is afraid of nothing. He just smiled. That's what he does when he doesn't feel like answering you.

It was from that day that Madillo and I really started to get to know Winifred. Before it had mainly been just the two of us, and sometimes Fred – but he's really a home friend. We get on with the others in the class, but it's hard to make new friends, because – well, we have each other and often that is enough. Sometimes too much. But now we have Winifred. She has made school more interesting, and it's funny that our two best friends are both Freds, in different ways.

Winifred has also made us like PE a little more than we did. Not a whole lot more – I don't think that will ever happen – but a little. Madillo and I don't really like PE. It's not because we're lazy, it's just that things like netball don't really excite us. Madillo hates that you have to stand still when you have the ball. Also, if you're not one of the best in the team then the others don't really pass it to you, which is especially boring. Winifred changed all that. She is one of the best at netball, so she always has the ball, and when she gets it she passes it to us. Because she does that, the others now do it as well, as if they imagine that we're good because Winifred thinks so. So we're trying to get a bit better, just so we don't let her down.

When I got to school this morning, I decided I had to speak to her. It was worse than ever. Her eyes were all puffed up and red – she had definitely been crying.

I don't think I have ever seen anyone look so sad.

Winifred is full Zambian, not half-and-half like me and Madillo. Dad says I mustn't say half-and-half, I must say I am a two hundred per cent child – one hundred per cent Bemba and one hundred per cent Irish. But that's too long and there's nothing wrong with half-and-half, because added together two halves make a whole, just a more interesting one. Winifred is Bemba-speaking, even though a lot of people in Lusaka speak Nyanja. Her dad, who is dead now, came from the Northern Province, like our dad. I suppose her mum did as well. She is still alive, thank goodness. I wouldn't like to think of Winifred being an orphan. They live in Kalingalinga, which is not far from us.

Their house has two rooms, and in it live Winifred and her mother as well as the uncle that she hates and some other children who are related to her – but I don't know them. I cannot bear to think what it would be like if Dad died and then an uncle came and took his place. And my dad's brothers are actually nice. Winifred says her uncle has a very loud voice and drinks a lot of beer.

I don't know how she manages to arrive at school every day so neat and tidy or get her homework done when she lives in such a crowded house. And still she gets nothing wrong. When I said this to Madillo earlier, she reminded me that this was before the evil spirit took over her body and mind. By this stage the evil spirit had acquired a name – Minuminu, which in Bemba means "blind snake". In Madillo's imagination I am sure it even has a mother and father and a couple of brothers and sisters. They are probably, in her mind, sitting down at a table inside Winifred having a nice cup of tea. Madillo has no limits.

Anyway, when the bell rang for breaktime I asked Winifred if she would come and sit with me. She nodded but then said, "Don't start asking me questions, Bul-Boo. Not today." So that was my talking plan gone. I was relieved in a way, because I didn't really know how to ask her what was wrong without seeming nosy.

We live about a mile away from Winifred, on Twin Palms Road. The palms around there are called "pregnant palms" (not their Latin name, but a good description as they all have a bulge in the middle). Coconut palms might have been more exciting, but Zambia is pretty far from the sea and they prefer the sea air. At least that is what Dad says. He often talks about plants that way, as if they are people. I close my eyes sometimes and imagine the pregnant palms making their clumsy way down the road, bending their heads towards one another as they chat about their cousins enjoying the sea air so far away.

Our house has many more than two rooms – I would have to count them up in my head to work out the right number. And we have a garden. When Winifred comes here she loves being in the garden and says she would like just one of the big trees to be transplanted into her yard, then she could sit under it in the afternoons, sheltered from the sun, and do her homework. When she comes over to us we never spend any time inside. Mum makes us food and we spread a blanket outside so we can eat there, under the shade of the flame tree. That is Winifred's favourite one.

After we discovered that we both knew the Snake Man, we also worked out that our dads were from the same place. Before that she had not known that we could speak Bemba. Ours is not perfect like Winifred's because we speak mostly English at home. Bemba has a nice sound to it: it is a round language, not a square one. No hard corners on any of the words. Here's an example: a ghost in Bemba is a *mulungulwa* and a tsetse fly is a *kashembele*. If you compare that to German, where a ghost is a *geist* and a tsetse fly is a *tse-tse fliege,* you can see what I mean. Not to be horrible about German, it's just personal preference. For example, I would prefer to tell someone that I had just seen a *mulungulwa*. Sounds more mysterious.

I write down any words I like, in any language, in

my notebook. But the notebook is mainly for observations. I call my notebook *Obuza-ba's Observations on Life in General*. *Obuza-ba* means "observer" in Japanese and it is my name for myself when I don't feel like being Bul-Boo. My real name, Bul-Boo, means "kangaroo rat" in Aboriginal. Neither of my parents are Aboriginal; they have in fact never stepped foot in Australia. I have no grandparent called Bul-Boo. And as far as I'm concerned, I do not resemble either a kangaroo or a rat or a terrifying combination of both. My parents, in their wisdom, picked the name out of thin air, tossed it around a little and decided to plonk it onto me. They told me it was an international name, whatever that's supposed to mean. If you look on the bright side, it is unique – but whether that makes up for it I am not sure. That's why I gave myself another name, although I'm the only person who uses it. My notebook is very, very secret. Not even Madillo knows about it. Which is just as well, because sometimes I write things about her and Mum and Dad in it.

Like the day I made the mistake of saying to Dad that the best thing about being bitten by a tsetse fly would be that you'd get sleeping sickness and could lie in bed all day. I said that if it was me, I reckon he and Mum would try and coax me out of my sleep with large bowls of ice cream. Dad, who prides himself on being unafraid of the truth, said that it was not an entertaining or restful illness, and if you slept for long enough you would die. Plus, if I got it there's no way he'd be bringing me ice cream. So I stopped wishing for it. That day I wrote in my notebook: Sometimes I wish Mum and Dad were less devoted to the truth.

Bul-Boo

Today I was supposed to speak to Winifred. Again. She was at school, but she looked so sick and silent that I was afraid to speak to her. Tomorrow will be better. I noticed that she got most of her maths wrong. Well, to be precise, nine out of ten wrong. Something must be troubling her, she never usually gets even one wrong. I must remember not to tell Madillo, or she'll start off again on her spirit theories.

It's hard to get used to Winifred like this because she's usually the one who stops us from being grumpy. One day Madillo and I had a fight on the way to school, a really stupid fight. I had seen an *nsolo*, a bird that's called a honey guide because that's exactly what it does:

it leads animals and people to beehives so that after they have broken the hive open the honey guide can eat from it. Honey guides eat everything in the hive, even the wax. I love them. So I pointed this one out to Madillo. Now Madillo is more interested in things you can't see, things that I think mostly don't exist – spirits and the like. I'm interested in things you can see. So I know more than her about things like wildlife and birds and insects. But Madillo also likes to be right.

"That's not an *nsolo*, Bul-Boo," she said. "You don't get them in town. If they lived in town, how would they get to the hives? And even if they did, there are no honey badgers in town to break them up, so they would have nothing to guide. No hives, no badgers, no food – therefore, no honey-guide birds."

"It is! I saw it and heard it," I said.

"You're probably just imagining it. I think it was a drongo."

That is probably the only bird name she knows, apart from things like chickens or peacocks, so I shouldn't have got into an argument about it. I knew I was right, so it was pointless. Anyway, I did get into the argument, and by the time we arrived at school we weren't speaking. It was Winifred who put a stop to it by asking, "You were fighting about a *bird*?" as if she couldn't believe it. "A small thing like that?" Then she started leaping around us, flapping imaginary wings, which made us feel even sillier. We both got embarrassed at the same time, even though I had no reason to be because I wasn't the one who was wrong. And that was the end of the argument.

I think Madillo gets her stubbornness from Mum. But apart from Mum's stubborn streak – and the fact that she and Dad gave us slightly unusual names – our parents are OK. More than OK, really. If I had to choose parents, I'd choose them.

They can be a bit silly sometimes and Fred says they don't always act like real parents. He's one to talk – his own family is pretty weird – although he did say that after I told him about the time Mum decided to stop wearing shoes, so there's some excuse.

"People have been doing this for thousands of years," she'd said, kicking off her sandals. "Shoes are just a barrier between us and our world."

That's one way of looking at it, I suppose.

First off she blistered – big, puffy, watery blisters, the kind that are very tempting to pop, but she wouldn't let either of us touch them. Only Dad was allowed near them, because he's a doctor. (The fact that she is also a doctor had passed her by.) Then she got hookworm.

The dreaded hookworm. I know the hookworm journey off by heart. They literally worm their way in through the soles of your feet into your bloodstream then head straight for your lungs. They don't stay there too long, but wriggle towards your mouth, where you promptly swallow them. That's how they end up in your intestines. Once they get there, they suck your blood and lay eggs. They live for ten years and can lay up to ten thousand eggs a day. You do the maths. I wonder if Sister Leonisa has a cure for them as well.

I didn't intend for this to be a lecture about hook-worm. It must seem a strange way to introduce my parents. Anyway, their names are Sean and Lula, short for Tallulah. If that was my name, I wouldn't have shortened it. Mum doesn't even have to make up an interesting meaning for it: it means "leaping water" in Choctaw or "fruitful woman" in Gaelic. I would opt for the first meaning, as there is something a bit gross about the second. It makes me think of a large, round woman producing endless babies from under her voluminous skirts. Her smile is beatific (I have been waiting for an opportunity to use that word) as they crawl around her, mewling and puking. And yes, that is a stolen line – from Shakespeare, as it happens.

There's nothing too poetic about Dad's name. Sean is Gaelic for John, which means "God is gracious". If it had been "God is great", then in Arabic that would have been *Allahu akbar*, which literally translates into "God is greater than can possibly be described". That would have been verging on the edge of poetic (although I added in the word "possibly" for dramatic effect). But his name is just Sean. Even though he has an Irish name he is not Irish, he was named after an Irish priest who had lived in Zambia and who his parents must have liked. Dad left Zambia when he was eighteen after he got a scholarship to study in Dublin. It was at university there that he and Mum met. Mum once told us that it was love at first sight, and Madillo said, "Mum, we don't want to know." Which was true, really. They are just Mum and Dad – the thought of them as young lovers is too much.

We all moved to Zambia when Madillo and I were only small, about three years old. Mum says it was because Dad was homesick for Zambia and she wanted to do something useful with her life by going where doctors were actually needed. I'd imagine they are needed everywhere, but she is right really, because of AIDS. I think AIDS is one of the saddest diseases there is. That and cancer.

In Uganda they call AIDS "the slim disease", for obvious reasons. I know that there is treatment now, but it is so expensive that most people can't afford it. Dad says that people in Africa with AIDS get thin and then die, while in Europe and America people with AIDS

live pretty long lives. And they don't even get that thin.
There is nothing fair about that.

Ifwafwa

It was because of Winston that I left home. My mother told me that he would do to me what he had done to my grandmother if I stayed there. It was time for me to leave my mother's home; I was at an age where I could work and seek a wife.

I did not want to leave my mother on her own but she told me that Lesa, the sky god, would look after her. I told her it wasn't true. Lesa does not come down to meddle in our business but merely looks down from the sky and sees everything. The best we could hope for would be that he would kill Winston by sending a bolt of lightning down to him. He did not do that.

My mother would not listen to me, though, and sent

me away with my heart full of sadness and pain. She gave me this bicycle so I could travel where I wanted, but she stayed behind. I never saw her again, not alive and not dead. He killed her, in the same way that he killed my grandmother. And he took her body away and hid it. He hid it so that to this day we have never found it. One day, when I feel strong enough, I will go back there and I will find him. I will make him show me where he put them both. My friends, those that slither along the earth on their bellies, they will help me. Perhaps, for him, I can ask the pale one for help. Then Winston will not laugh at me or ask me, "Where is your grandmother's magic now?"

When he sees the pale snake coming out of my bag, there will be fear in his eyes. That is how it should be, because he, like all the others, does not believe that the pale one exists. The only time anyone believes is when they see it with their own eyes. Then it is too late. I will call upon my grandmother then, in his presence, and he will know fear. When I am strong enough.

Bul-Boo

Finally, today, I spoke to Winifred. And I was highly unsuccessful. I spoke to her at break but she wouldn't answer me when I asked if something was wrong. She kept looking around to see if anyone was watching us and then just stood staring down at the ground. She almost looked ashamed, as if she had done something that was so bad she couldn't even speak of it. Then she said I should leave her alone, she was tired. Winifred is never tired and doesn't know how to lie very well – she should ask Madillo for some lessons if she is going to start that now.

Later she went missing, just like that. I didn't see her go; I only noticed that she was not there. I asked Sister if Winifred had gone home and she told me, as I could have expected, that it was none of my business. I took that as a yes. I didn't know what to do then. I hope it wasn't my fault that she left.

Fred came round to our house after school and I decided to speak to him about Winifred. This, of course, meant that Madillo would be involved in the conversation and I'd run the risk of exposing Fred to the evil-spirit theory, but there was nothing I could do about that.

Fred lives next door to us. Apart from him, his family is not your average next-door type – you know, the kind who chat to you over the fence as they water their baby avocado trees, or who warn you about the puff adder in their garden that recently gave birth. (Given that puff adders can have eighty or more young ones and the babies come straight out of the mother ready for action, a warning would be neighbourly.)

Fred's mother is called Sarah. She is from somewhere in England, I'm not sure where. She is very small and so shy that I have never once heard her speak. For all I know, she could have a big, deep voice inside her little body. Or no voice at all. Madillo and I sometimes try to get her to speak to us over the fence by waving, giving her frights or asking her how she is. But we've heard no sound yet: she just smiles at us. She has a nice smile. She is always in the garden, working away, and she wears a big straw hat, almost like a sombrero. We call her Fungi-san – not loud enough for her to hear – but she does look like a mushroom wandering around their garden, popping up silently in unexpected places. (In Japanese you add *san* onto a name to show respect.)

Fred's dad, Meshack, is Zambian like our dad, but from a different part of the country. I would say he's almost twice the size of his wife. In fact he is probably as wide as she is tall. He is more talkative than she is – not really hard, I suppose, to talk more than a silent person – and he always greets us. Because he's so tall, he can spot us from anywhere in their garden and he shouts out, "Hey, twin. I can see you," which can be a little unnerving, especially if you are at the top of the kapok tree. It is a very tall tree and very leafy. And I know that all trees have leaves, but this one seems to have more than most. If you wore green, there's no way anyone could see you. Anyone but Fred's dad, that is.

One day we were sitting right in the middle of the tree and Madillo said to me, "I bet you fifty kwacha that Meshack 'extraterrestrial perception' Mwamba will see us here. Watch him: he'll stand in the middle of the garden with his eyes closed and still he'll see us."

I took the bet because Madillo always thinks that people have undisclosed powers. Unlike me, she doesn't rate evidence very highly. What's more, I have explained to her many times that there is no such thing as extra-terrestrial perception – it is extra*sensory* (if it even exists) – but she won't listen. And as Meshack always wears sunglasses, we wouldn't be able to see whether his eyes were open or closed. As it happened, we had hardly shaken hands on the bet when we heard him: "Hey, twins, get out of that big tree, there could be a green mamba waiting for you." Then he laughed. It was almost as if he had heard us talking about him.

We came down, and I lost fifty kwacha.

Between them, Meshack and Sarah have two children: Fred and Joseph. Both of them are boys, although Madillo thinks the youngest one, Joseph, is a hermaph-rodite. She only thinks that because of an article she read in the *New Scientist* and because she likes the notion of hermaphrodites. As you may have guessed, I have explained to her that there is no such thing as a human hermaphrodite. Chimera, yes; hermaphrodite, no. If Joseph (Fred's eight-year-old brother) was a worm, then she may have a point. But he isn't.

Fred is where this all started. He's the best person in the whole of Zambia – in fact, maybe in the whole of Africa. Madillo's theory on this is that he is actually not Meshack and Sarah's child. She didn't go so far as to say he was a changeling, just that there could have been a mix-up in the hospital. It does happen, I know. And I kind of like the theory because he is so different from the whole lot of them. But it's hard to get over the fact that Fred looks like someone who came out of a shake-up of his mum and his dad.

Then there is his great-granny, who I've mentioned already. Fred says that she lives with them because if she had stayed in the village, being a famous witch and all that, the other villagers might have killed her. Well, what he actually said was, "They would have torn her limb from limb and thrown her body to the lions." I don't know how he came up with that, but any time I see her, a ghastly image of her being torn limb from limb comes into my head. The thought of having a witch as our neighbour thrills Madillo, and if she ever sees her in the garden she lowers her head – "Respect for the witch," she says. To me she is just a funny, very old lady.

When Fred came over this afternoon, we went down to our spot at the bottom of the garden. I had told Madillo it was only fair that I got to tell him the story, as it's me Winifred sits next to – and anyway, I was the one who first noticed that something was wrong. My main reason for insisting on this was so I could get the right version through to Fred.

When I had finished telling him, he just sat there

looking puzzled. When Fred looks puzzled, his whole face screws up.

"I thought you were going to tell me something exciting... This is nothing. Nothing has happened except that Winifred doesn't put her hand up any more and she looks down at the ground when you speak to her."

"Well," I said, "it's just that she's changed, and so quickly that we think something is very wrong. She doesn't even smile any more. There has to be something wrong with that, doesn't there?"

Enter Madillo. "There does, and I think I know what it is. One of the things we're thinking is that her body has been taken over by an evil spirit."

We?

Fred's eyes slowly started to open. "Ah," he said, as if suddenly my boring story had become an interesting one.

Give Madillo an audience and there's no stopping her. "Yes – she shows all the signs of it. Yesterday I saw her sitting at her desk and her head began to loll to one side. I didn't see her face, but it was probably contorted—"

"Madillo! Don't lie," I protested.

"Calm down, Bul-Boo."

Madillo knows there is nothing I hate more in the world than to be told to calm down. "You weren't in the classroom at the time so you don't know."

She turned back to Fred. "I have sometimes seen Winifred walking and it looks like she has some kind of limp: she drags her left leg slightly, as if something is pulling on it. I was wondering if we should speak to your great-granny about it. Does she have exorcist powers? Because I'm not sure that all witches do."

Before Fred could answer, I stood up, tired of listening to all this. "Do I need to remind you that this is one of our best friends you're talking about? I wish I'd not told either of you. Winifred is upset about something and all you care about is proving some crazy evil-spirit thing. I don't want you to speak to anyone about it. I'm going to find out what's wrong and then decide what to do. You can help then if you want to. You should care about her, Fred, as she has half your name." (Stupid thing to say, I know, but I was mad.)

Fred laughed. "You get so cross, Boo. You should do what my mum does: breathe in deep, then hold your breath, then breathe out. I'm sorry, anyway. I'll listen now."

I tried hard to imagine Fred's silent mum breathing in deeply. I could almost imagine that, but not her getting angry in the first place. What would she do? Stare angrily at the person? Have a big, silent tantrum? Then breathe deeply?

"I won't get angry if we can have a proper conversation that doesn't involve non-existent things. And her head did *not* loll, Madillo – that's just you." I found it hard to stay cross with either of them, so the fight didn't last long. But it did make them stop with the possession talk.

At the end of it all we decided that I should try and speak to Winifred again the next day, and the next, and even the next, until she eventually answered my question. If that didn't work then we'd make another plan.

After that discussion I wrote a small but very useful observation in my notebook: When Madillo lies, she talks a little louder and scratches the back of her neck. If she thinks you really, really know she is lying, she will eventually just stop arguing about it.

Bul-Boo

This is what I wrote in my notebook today: There are some things that are so awful you wish you had not heard them. Ever. What Winifred told me today is one of those things.

I was not prepared in any which way for what Winifred told me. And she could see that when she said the words. I did not know what to say or where to look. That made it worse for her, I know that, but I couldn't help myself. It is too awful. I don't know what I was prepared for, but I think even the evil-spirit explanation might have been easier to accept.

It was my third day of trying to get her to talk to me. I think she just gave in because I kept pestering her and following her around. Eventually she turned to me and I could see she was crying. Big, slow tears were running from her eyes. "Bul-Boo," she said, "I will tell you. But there's nothing we can do about it."

She turned away and I followed her. She walked towards the corner of the playground. No one else was there. Then she crouched on the ground and began to speak, keeping her voice low and quiet. I had to crouch next to her to make sure I heard properly.

"My father died – you know that, Bul-Boo – he died last year. My father loved me," she added, wiping her eyes with the sleeve of her shirt. "Nothing has ever been the same since then, and each day it gets worse. It is my uncle's fault. My uncle, who forced my mother… It's tradition, she tells me: the brother takes what has been left behind… But it's not tradition for him to carry on staying after that first night."

It was difficult to follow what she was saying, but I didn't want to interrupt.

"My uncle says that now his brother – my father – is dead, he's my mother's husband. So he came to her on the night of the burial and has never left. But I don't think she loves him, Bul-Boo; she's scared of him. And he drinks all the time."

Winifred looked at me as if I should say something, but I couldn't. My mind was too full.

"Last month my mother said to me that now I'm becoming a woman, it is time to start thinking about marriage."

"What?" I said disbelievingly. "Marriage? You?"

She hung her head low, unable to look at me, and I immediately regretted my words. Her voice came out in a whisper. "Yes, Bul-Boo... Now, very soon. I heard my mother telling my uncle that it isn't right: we're in the town now, we have left all that behind. But he said no, we will never leave it behind. The way of the village. It is him making all this happen, he's forcing my mother. She repeats his words to me but her eyes show me she doesn't believe them. She looks like someone who's lying."

I didn't reply. I couldn't.

"The other day," Winifred continued, "my uncle's friend came to the house – the old man with the large stomach who I've told you about before. He goes to the tavern with my uncle and they drink together. I always hide away when they come back. This day he walked straight into the room where I was and looked at me. He rubbed his hands together slowly, like this, and he said, 'Soon you will be coming with me.' I ran out of the room, Bul-Boo, to my mother in the kitchen—"

She stopped suddenly as the bell rang and stood

up. "We must go now. I'll talk to you later." Then she turned and left.

I watched Winifred go. She's like me, not even tall for her age. Maybe she was confused; had it all wrong. It could be that she only *thought* that's what he'd said. Maybe her mother was just giving her "the talk" that we all dreaded.

Mum tried that with us but it didn't work. One day she said, "Girls," (she only says that when she is about to tell us something we don't want to hear) "there are a few things we should really talk about." I didn't even have to answer, because Madillo just looked at her and said, "Not today, Mum. Not even tomorrow or the next day. If it's what I think it is. We know everything already."

That was definitely an exaggeration but I think Mum didn't really know what to say to it, so she let it pass. (She doesn't usually give up too easily, so she'll be back.) Maybe that's what Winifred's mother was trying to talk to her about and Winifred didn't hear her properly.

I walked slowly back to class through the playground, not knowing how to face Winifred after what she had told me. This was much, much worse than I'd thought. This wasn't just Winifred being a bit upset. I would talk to her again on the way back from school.

She didn't say anything to me during class, or to

anyone. Sister didn't even try to ask her a question, it was as if she had given up on her. After school I waited while she packed her bag. She always takes longer than anyone else because she is so tidy.

"Is this all true, Winifred?" I said.

She stopped packing her books for a minute and looked at me. "It's true. I'm promised to that old man. I'm going to be his wife and live with him in his house – his mother's house – far from here, out of town some-where. My uncle will have his way: I'll be gone from his house. And no more school." I saw her hands were shaking.

"Winifred, we have to stop this. It can't happen. We'll do something."

"What are you going to do? There's nothing to be done. It is only four weeks away." Her voice broke.

"I'll speak to my dad, he'll do something. We'll hide you where they can't find you. We'll tell the police—"

"He's a policeman himself, this ugly old man – it's no use," she said, crying now.

The caretaker arrived just then to lock up the classroom. "Move out now, school's finished," he said, shaking his keys at us. We both jumped and then grabbed our bags, remembering the story of how he'd once locked two girls in the school for the night because they didn't leave fast enough.

When we reached Twin Palms Road, Winifred and I went our separate ways, her to the right and me to the left. My stomach was swirling as I watched her walk away. I would tell Dad; he would think of something.

Ifwafwa

I visit all the houses in this town. The big ones with trees and swimming pools and the small ones that are sometimes blown away in the storms. I am welcome in all of them because I take the snakes with me when I leave. Nobody turns me away. Nobody asks me questions about how I do it. They are grateful. And my gift is growing. My grandmother told me that a gift does not stay the same; you must use it well. You must practise and then you will get better. If you do not use it, you will find one day that it will turn against you. I did not want that to happen. So I carried on practising. She was right. There is no snake any more that can resist me. Not even the gaboon viper.

I never used to see it around town; it stayed near the trees in the land that lies low. Not like here in Lusaka, where we sit so high above the sea that I think it is easy for Lesa to watch over us. But now the viper comes here. Everyone is afraid of it, the snake with the little horns on its nose. The snake with the bags of poison that never run out. The snake that could bite many people and kill every one of them. But it doesn't bite unless it has no choice. The people fear it because of these bags, but it is a quiet, kind snake. The easiest for me to catch. It never runs from me.

The only snake that troubles me, that I do not properly understand, is the white one with the pale, pale stomach. But I am taking my time with it. One day that, too, will obey me.

My grandmother practised her gift all her life. It was a gift that made people fearful of her. She could start a fire just by thinking about it, she did not even have to think hard or be close to where she wanted it to start. Once she told me that she just had to see the place in her mind and the flames would appear. Everyone in our village knew this, which is why they feared her. No one wanted a fire to start in their home or, worse, on their bodies. She had been known to do that only once, when the elders were teaching the young girls about becoming women. At night these girls would be kept away from everyone in a hut on the edge of the village. One night – I do not know how my grandmother knew of this – an old man was creeping towards the hut with bad ideas in his head.

Suddenly out of nowhere he started burning. He woke everyone with his screams as he rolled in the dirt, trying to put out the flames. They took much longer to go out than normal flames and he was scarred for ever. He was also filled with shame and I never saw him smile again.

My grandmother's gift failed her at the end of her life. I still do not know why.

Bul-Boo

I didn't tell Dad today, as I thought maybe I should speak to Fred and Madillo about it first. I called Fred through the hedge and he came over to sit with Madillo and me. I am still not sure it was a good idea to tell them, but anyway, I did.

Fred arrived with his hair full of leaves and twigs. He always comes through the hedge. He says that his mum does not particularly notice whether he is there or not, so it doesn't matter which way he comes, it's just he prefers that way.

Before I started, I made them both promise that they would not interrupt me or even mention evil spirits or head-lolling. They promised: Madillo with closed eyes and her face raised to the sky and Fred as usual muttering the words under his breath. He's never liked being told what to do, so he pretends it's not happening.

"I finally spoke to Winifred," I said, "and she is in a terrible, terrible situation. We have to help her. Her uncle is forcing her to marry an old man in four weeks' time. He says it is tradition … Bemba tradition."

Madillo let out a gasp but then remembered her promise.

"Even Winifred's mother is involved, planning this with the uncle, although Winifred says it's because she is scared of him." I stopped for a minute, as I heard a rustle in the grass on the other side of the hedge. "Did you hear that?" I asked.

They shook their heads silently.

I listened again but the noise had stopped. Maybe it was a cat coming in off the road.

"We have four weeks to do something. Winifred says we can't go to the police because this old man is a policeman. But I think we should at least tell Dad, maybe he can speak to someone. Winifred's mother is from the same village as Dad's mum, after all. What do you think?"

Madillo gestured to me as if she had been struck dumb by the God of Silence and was waiting for the curse to be lifted.

"Speak, O quiet one," I said, happy to oblige.

"What about speaking to Fred's great-granny? Now I know you said we shouldn't talk about witches and that kind of thing, but ask Fred about the things she has solved ... go on, ask him."

Reluctantly I turned to Fred. "Well?"

"Lots of things, really," he said. "She is known to be a very powerful witch." Then he sat back, as if that was all that needed to be said.

In some ways he was right.

"What would we ask your great-granny to do? Put a spell on the old man?"

He shrugged. "I don't know. I've never asked her to do anything before ... especially not in a case like this. Maybe she could make him disappear?"

"Well," said Madillo, "that wouldn't be any use if the uncle was still around, he'd just find somebody else for her to marry."

She had a point. And it was logical. Must make a note of that: Today Madillo used logic.

"It would probably be simpler if we just got rid of the uncle," she continued. "There'd be nothing the old man could do then."

Just then the hedge moved again and I jumped up and peered through it. I *knew* I had heard something. And there was Ifwafwa leaning against the hedge, fast asleep, his bag of snakes on his stomach. I wouldn't wake him, but seeing him did give me an idea. What if we spoke to him about it? Maybe *he* would know what to do.

"Shh…" I motioned to the others. "Ifwafwa is out there, fast asleep."

Fred crept over on his hands and knees to check.

"What if he heard us?" Madillo said.

"He would never tell anyone, you know what he's like. But I think we should tell him anyway. We won't use Winifred's name – as he knows her – just explain the situation and ask him for advice."

"Before we ask Fred's—"

"I think so. It's safer. If she does have all these … powers, we should be careful about unleashing them." I doubted she had even one power, but I preferred the option of talking to Ifwafwa.

There was little point in waiting for Ifwafwa to wake up, he sleeps deeper than anyone I have ever seen, so we left him in peace and decided we would check on him each hour. We had got used to the fact that a bag of snakes, all of them probably poisonous, would lie peacefully on his stomach for as long as he slept.

He has tried to persuade me many times to make friends with the snakes, but I can't. I agreed to touch a small python once, but only because it was too small to squeeze me to death. I wouldn't touch any of the others in his bag. I never understand how all of them can be in there together and not fight with each other. Imagine if it was a bag of humans: they would fight from the minute they got inside.

Ifwafwa

I have many memories, many ancient voices, in my head. As I move around from place to place, sometimes it is hard for me to remember where I am now. There is no longer anywhere I call my home. When I go back to where I was born, it will be with hatred and grieving in my heart. I am taking so long to get there because I do not want it to be that way, but I cannot help the way things are.

I left my mother there alone, she could not even seek comfort and strength from the graveside of my grandmother, who lay unburied. And now she, too, lies unburied. I was not there to bury her, my own mother, and I can feel that her spirit is unhappy because of it.

The man who killed her would have thrown her to one side, not caring whether or not her head faced east towards our ancestors. There would have been no one there to purify her home and make way for her spirit to return. I do not know where she wanders now; when she comes to me, she is far from home. Lonely. I cannot help her. It is his doing.

But my grandmother's spirit is stronger than her killer's. She comes to me without fear. Last night she told me that his heart is weak and that he lies in his hut all day, waiting for death. Maybe the time to go home is coming soon.

Bul-Boo

Ifwafwa took two hours to wake up, and already the sun was starting to go down. I didn't have much time to tell him the story, but he understands things so quickly you never have to use too many words. Unlike Madillo, he never interrupts you. He listens with his head held slightly to one side, and his brown eyes look straight at you. He is very easy to talk to. I decided not to tell him any names and he did not mind.

"Ifwafwa, today I have a story for you, but it is a story with no names. A real story. And I want you to tell me what to do."

He nodded, so slightly you would hardly have known it was a nod.

"I have a friend, a young girl, the same age as me. She's Bemba-speaking. Last year her father died, and her uncle moved in the same day. He is now her mother's husband. This girl doesn't like the uncle and misses her father. And the uncle – who is not a nice man – has now decided that she is to be married to his friend, an old man who drinks too much Chibuku and who looks at her in a wrong way." I watched Ifwafwa to see what he was thinking, but I could see only his kind face waiting for me to go on.

"She's too young to get married but her mother won't help her as she's scared of the uncle. My friend cries a lot and can't do her schoolwork. I don't know how to help her. What should I do?"

Ifwafwa lowered his eyes and was silent for a few minutes. Then he spoke. "I will need to have a think about this, Bul-Boo. A long think. You see, it's hard when people misuse tradition. This uncle does not sound like a respectful man. It is no use if a wife is scared of the man she has accepted as a husband. If this girl's mother is scared, then this thing will not work. I will think about it, and when I know what to do I will come back to you."

He shook my hand, as he always does, and his hands felt warm and dry like the snakes he loves. He said he wasn't hungry, so he didn't come to eat at our house.

I was not sure if he was telling me the truth, because he looked so thin. Madillo once said that maybe he eats the snakes that he takes from the houses. That he only pretends to like them. But I know that's not true. She knows it's not true as well, it is just that she likes the sound of the stories she tells.

I watched Ifwafwa once in our house without him knowing. (He never lets anyone into the room with him when he's catching snakes because he says they sense people's fear and will not come out.) He had come to us because we had discovered a puff adder in the lounge downstairs. There are big doors leading out from the room into the garden, and just outside them is a huge honeysuckle creeper. I crept in behind that and watched him. Ifwafwa walked into the middle of the room and lay down flat on his back, closing his eyes. He stretched his arms out each side of him and lay perfectly still. From my position I could not even be sure whether he was breathing or not. This went on for a while and then I saw the puff adder slide out slowly from underneath the couch, almost as if it wanted to get a better look at the small man.

Still he did not move. Then I heard a noise coming from his still figure. It was not like the singing he does when he carries the snakes around, more like a low hum. He knew the snake was watching him. When that noise started, it was almost as if an invisible string was pulling the snake towards him. It just moved steadily and slowly towards him and then went and laid its head on his outstretched hand.

It was hard not to scream. I thought it was about to strike and then Ifwafwa would die on our stone floor, killed by one of the creatures he loved best. But it was not so. Still humming, he rolled over so his face was only centimetres from the snake's head. It was then that he saw me. He did not stop his noise, nor did he move, but I saw from his eyes that I should leave. Which I did. He never spoke about it to me and this made me feel worse than if he had shouted. I've never told anyone about it.

When Iwafwa had finished that day, he told Dad that he had found another, smaller puff adder, and so he took them both away. He said they were brothers. How on earth he could tell that from looking at them, I don't know. If I was to put twelve puff adders in a row, there's no way I could tell which ones were related.

I decided I wouldn't tell Winifred that I had spoken to anyone. I'd wait a bit and see what Ifwafwa came up with. If he can't think of anything, I might have to ask Dad. Although Dad doesn't like interfering in other people's business, so maybe that won't work. He says that he wouldn't want anyone interfering in his.

He would put on what Madillo calls his resigned face and probably mumble something about tradition (even though, it seems to me, he doesn't stick to too many traditions himself).

I don't care how old a tradition is if it's something that hurts people. Just because something is old, that doesn't make it good. It was a tradition in China to bind young girls' feet into lumps of uselessness. Why should that be respected? It used to be tradition in England to make small children climb up the chimneys to clean them and then they would die from all the soot. That's no good for anyone at all.

Ifwafwa

I heard the three children talking. The one I know best told them the story of small Winifred. I know her and her mother. Her father died of the illness no one wants to name. He was from my home, near Mpika. He was not an old man; he died many years before his time was up. He died so thin that his bones shone through his skin and his head was a skull with his sad face stretched over it. When he died he left his wife, helpless, to be stamped on by his brother. His brother is not a good man. His head may be wide like a buffalo but there is much empty space inside it. He grunts and roars and uses words that are ugly. He has no respect. This friend of his, the one who wants to marry a child, cannot walk straight because his belly is round from beer. He has no business with small Winifred.

I knew a young girl like her once, in the village I can no longer call home. They called her Lubilo. The fast one. It was her they would send to catch the chickens, because they could not escape from her. When it was decided that she should marry the old one, she ran away from the village. She was gone before anyone knew. But she was taken by the crocodile when she stopped to drink water. I know this from the snakes who live by the edge of the river, the ones who watch from both sides of their heads. She was not fast enough to escape the crocodile who lies so still that he looks like stone.

Bul-Boo

I know that it was foolish to tell Madillo. She keeps a promise only until she forgets she made it. Sometimes she forgets within minutes. At supper, I knew she was going to say something even before she opened her mouth. She has this way of looking at you from the sides of her eyes without even turning her head. Then comes the deep breath. I think there's a voice inside her head saying, "You probably shouldn't be doing this, Madillo, but you've started now, so carry on…"

"Mum, are there forced marriages all over the world?" she asked.

"Not *all* over the world, but in some places, yes. Some work, some don't."

That was a very un–Mum–like response. Short, no lecture on how women everywhere are oppressed and how this is just one example. Maybe she was hungry and didn't feel like using up her eating time.

It gave me a glimmer of hope that this would be the end of it. Maybe, in some other Madillo-free universe, it might have been.

"Dad…?"

"Yes, little one," he said, oblivious to the narrowed eyes of Madillo on a mission.

"Do you think that the Bemba-speaking people are good?"

He laughed. "Bemba-speaking people? Like me, and you, and your sister?"

"Yes."

"Well, there's good and bad in everyone. I wouldn't say one group has all the good in the world, nor all the bad."

"Well, the traditions … are they good?"

"Which traditions? There are thousands of things that could be called traditions," he said.

Time to intervene.

"We're studying tradition with Sister Leonisa at school … in history," I said quickly.

"Why does she assume that all traditions of the Bemba fall into the 'historical' category? I might have to have a word with her," Dad said.

From past experience I know that "I might have to have a word with her" means it has already been decided that many more than one word will be exchanged with Sister Leonisa.

"I didn't finish what I was saying, Dad," I said in the humblest voice possible. "I meant history *and* geography…"

Madillo seemed to be enjoying my misery here.

"Well, in either subject, why does the question of good or bad arise? And are you studying the traditions of, say, the English-speaking people of the world? Or does Sister Leonisa think that only people in Africa have traditions worth studying?"

Just when I thought we had avoided a lecture from Mum, Dad was getting into full swing.

"Well," Madillo said, undeterred. "Say, for example, the way young girls are forced to marry old men… Surely that's not good?"

So much for my diversion.

Dad finally put down his fork and paid proper attention. "That is not good, no. But it's something that's in decline. You wouldn't find it in town any more, only in the villages."

"Not true," muttered Madillo, just loud enough to be heard.

"Is there something you wanted to say, Dilly? In a voice we can all hear?"

Madillo hates it when Mum uses the shortened version of her name. Never mind being named after an armadillo, she once told me that being called "Dilly" makes her feel like a small cow with a bell round her neck.

The advantage of Mum calling her this was that Madillo then refused to continue the conversation – on principle, she said, because Mum knows how she feels about the name. I was glad, I just felt embarrassed at the thought of what Winifred would say if she knew her life was being discussed over supper.

Ifwafwa

It rained today after I left the girls' house. Big heavy drops of rain that filled the potholes in the road and washed away the heat of the day. I had far to go because the bag was full and the snakes were restless. They grow tired of being trapped in the bag, they want to move along the ground and feel the wet against their bodies and then, when the rain stops, find rocks warmed up by the sunshine.

In the rainy season I am busy, but in the dry, cold season the snakes sleep the long sleep. Then it is quiet and people have no need for the Snake Man. Sometimes they forget about me until September, when the wake-up begins. Then they remember. In the sleeping months

I travel away from the high land of Lusaka, down to where it is warmer. There I can rest and still find food. Only a little, but if I keep very still the food lasts long.

Since I left home, food has not mattered to me so much. Never again will I taste the *nshima* porridge that my mother made for me when I was small. Soft and warm in my stomach. Now food is just whatever I can find. The only food that I can taste properly in my heart is a sweet mango. Every time I bite into one I can see my mother looking up at the mango tree, waiting for them to ripen. Not one would she let fall to the ground.

Bul-Boo

Because I wasn't sure if I could wait for Ifwafwa to think about this, I decided to tell Dad about Winifred today. Ifwafwa is a kind man but he has sleepy eyes. Everything he does, he does slowly. (Maybe that's why the snakes like him, because he never gives them a fright.) There isn't much time left for Winifred, and if Ifwafwa has a long, slow think about everything it will be too late.

However, telling Dad did not go exactly as planned. He comes back early on a Wednesday, so he was home by the time we got in from school. I did not especially want Madillo with me but she always knows when I am trying to avoid her. Even if I try not to act suspiciously. Today was just like that.

"What are you doing when we get home?" she said after counting her steps in Bemba (she is taking a break from Japanese). Numbers in Bemba can get very long (twenty-one, for example, is *makumi yabili na cimo* – which, if you translated it, would be "two times ten and one", so it took us even longer than usual to get home). And to add to it Madillo only knows numbers up to a hundred, so it was very boring because she repeated herself at least ten times.

"Nothing in particular. Why?" I said.

"Are you sure you have nothing planned?"

"No." If I had said anything else, it would have been even more obvious. And "Why are you asking?" would have made me sound guilty.

"So … if you have nothing planned, you can help me pick mulberries. I'm going to dye my T-shirts mulberry colour. The best berries are at the top of the tree and I can't do it on my own."

"I'm tired, Madillo. I just want to lie down when we get home. Can I help you tomorrow? Or you could get Fred to help?"

"Why would I do that when I have you, my very own DNA? And anyway, Fred doesn't like mulberries so he won't want to touch them. He says they are devil food."

That is true. Fred has developed a category of food

he calls "devil food", and once he's put something in that category he will not eat it or even touch it. He says that if he touches it, it will creep in through his skin and then he'll be in the grip of the devil. He's spent too much time with Madillo. And his great-granny backs him up, so when he doesn't feel like eating something, he makes sure she is within hearing distance. Apparently she always says, "Listen to the poor boy. He's right: you must not make him eat that." His mum and dad seem to obey her, so it's easy for him to get his way when she's around.

"Well, what's the hurry, anyway? Tomorrow will do, won't it?"

"No, tomorrow is Thursday."

"And?"

"You can't pick mulberries on a Thursday, because…" Madillo looked around, trying to think of something. "Because bad things happen on a Thursday and then you might die in the tree."

Apart from anything else, I wasn't aware it had been decided I would be the one to climb the tree.

"On a Thursday in particular?"

"Well, Thursday's named after Thor. He's the one who throws lightning bolts from the sky, and it's the rainy season. Just think about it. I mean, if you want to die a horrible, flaming death in a mulberry tree, that's fine by me. I'm only thinking of you, Bul-Boo."

I wish I had not been "blessed" (as Mum says) with a vivid imagination, because despite knowing that not a word of this was true I suddenly saw myself crying out piteously as I tumbled to the ground, a whirling mass of flame and lightning bolt. An imagination like that is not a blessing. And I knew then that a large part of this afternoon would be spent picking mulberries. Which it was. I didn't mind really, because we've been picking them ever since we were small. Not the ones at the top that we can reach now, but the ones that hang down from the lower branches. Mum wrote a poem about it once, when we were about three. Here it is:

Mulberry Juice

They appeared at the back door,
Small bare bodies smudged.
"Look, we changed colour."
I looked.
Smeary purple smiles,
Delighted hands held up for my attention,
Bellies full and round.
Behind them I saw the tree,
Heavy with fruit and bright wide leaves.
The mulberries were finally ripe.

Anyway, I ended up not telling Dad, which was maybe just as well.

Ifwafwa

I think this time I must act fast. But I cannot tell the small girl what is to be done. She is quiet, but her sister talks to the wind if it will listen. She talks to the acacia trees and the stones, and to the snakes when they are carefully tied up in the bag. And if there is a human close to her, she will talk to them. If I tell the quiet one, she will tell her sister — and she will tell someone else. She cannot help it: they are one person split into two. There are some things children do not need to know and this is one of those things.

For this I will have to call on Chitimukulu, our great chief. Our priest who knows all things. He knows of my gift with the snakes, he knows I use it well. But I will seek his approval for what I must do. I do not want to bring shame to the Palace of Lubemba. Our tradition is not for abuse by old men with nothing but wickedness in their minds. It is not for buffalo heads and drunkards to destroy our young girls. I will speak to him and he will grant me permission.

The young girl who ran away – Lubilo, the fast one – she died in sadness and fear. Her small life was swallowed by the crocodile, which knows no better. Winifred walks now with a weight on her shoulders, her small head dropping so that she stares at the earth. But there is no hope for her in the earth. Perhaps she would rather die like Lubilo, quickly, with no time for thoughts. But I do not want that to happen. Chitimu-kulu would not want that to happen.

I must do this thing.

Bul-Boo

It was so hot last night, I couldn't sleep. All the windows were open but the air wasn't moving, so I got up and woke Madillo. This is not an easy thing to do – she could sleep through a tidal wave – but I didn't want to go downstairs by myself. Once I did that and I almost stepped on a scorpion that was just sitting at the bottom of the stairs as if it was waiting for me. I know some people say that scorpions won't attack you unless you attack them first, but how do they know the difference between an attack and someone stepping on them by mistake? I read about one type called the deathstalker, which definitely sounds like it would attack first. Although I suppose it didn't give itself that name. Anyway, that's why I woke Madillo to come with me.

When we got downstairs, I opened the fridge so I could stand in its cold air for a bit. We didn't switch on the lights or the mosquitoes would have come. Madillo just sat at the kitchen table and rested her head on her arms. I didn't need her falling asleep, so I decided (why do I always do this?) to talk to her about the back-up plan I had been thinking about.

"You know you suggested we spoke to Fred's great-granny about Winifred? Well, I think we should. It's not that I believe in this witch thing or anything, but maybe she can help."

Madillo sat up then. "I knew I was right. Did Fred ever tell you about the time she put a spell on the chief in their village? He had taken one of her goats without asking, and when she asked for it back he said he was the chief and it was now his goat. She cast a spell on him then and there – 'Abracadabra, psika psoka, hocus pocus, ying yong yang' – and he began to grow horns straight out of his head. Goats' horns, curly and hard, pushing their way through his skull. He begged her to take away the curse, he brought herds of goats to her door, he wailed and lay flat out on the ground in front of her. But she ignored him. And the horns carried on grow-ing, each day a few centimetres longer, until they were too heavy for his head and he could no longer stand upright." She stopped and looked at me. "So I think we should speak to her. Maybe she could cast a spell on this old man who wants to marry Winifred?"

"*Psika psoka, hocus pocus, ying yong yang*? Madillo, she did not say that! I know she didn't."

"Well, maybe not those exact words… But she did curse him – she has powers."

"What happened to the chief afterwards, did the horns stop growing?"

"When it got to the stage where he couldn't get up from the ground, she reversed the spell so that slowly, centimetre by centimetre, they shrank. But first she took his whole herd of goats, as well as his chickens and a cow. He never did anything to her again."

"Perhaps it would be too dangerous to involve her. What if she got irritated with *us*? Can you imagine what she'd do?"

"We're Fred's friends – she wouldn't do anything to us. Anyway, I think she likes me," Madillo said.

"Then you can do the talking," I said, because I know the way it goes. We make plans and then when we get to the point of having to speak to someone, Madillo goes quiet and pushes me forward, or just looks the other way as if she has nothing to do with it.

"I'm not good at talking to adults," she said.

A feeble excuse, but we agreed in the end, as we always do, that I would do the talking. We would ask Fred to bring his great-granny to the gate tomorrow so we could speak to her. (We don't like going into the house because of his silent mum and loud-voiced dad.)

I felt a bit cooler after standing in front of the fridge all this time, so we went back to bed where I dreamt I'd grown hooves on my hands and feet and couldn't write so Sister Leonisa put me out of the classroom.

Madillo and I have been put out of the classroom so many times, I can't keep count. It's as if Sister Leonisa wakes up some mornings and thinks, yes, today I might just have to put one of the twins out of the classroom. It could be for anything, big or small. And to be honest, I don't really mind – I prefer to be outside than in the stuffy classroom.

Winifred has only been put out once, but it was for a funny thing. One day she brought in a string with three tiny cowbells tied onto it. One of the boys who sits in front of our desk is called David and he's really annoying because he spends all his time trying to get into Sister Leonisa's good books, especially by telling on people. I don't know why he carries on doing it, because Sister doesn't like tell-tales, but he doesn't seem to notice. I think he has what Mum would call a "mean streak", which I always imagine as a thin streak running down his body with thin little mean thoughts trapped inside it.

That day I watched as Winifred carefully tied the string with the cowbells onto the back of David's trousers. She had wrapped the bells in tissue paper so they wouldn't make a noise while she tied the string. She's the only one who could have done it without him noticing, as she always does everything quietly. When David got up to go and tell on somebody, the bells started tinkling as if he had a ringing tail. That was when Winifred got put out of the class. And she felt bad about it – even though David's mean – so the next day she brought him a lollipop to say sorry. I think it's probably the only time I have seen her play a trick on someone. It stopped him telling tales, anyway, and since the lollipop he and Winifred have even become a bit friendly. Maybe he was just mean because he didn't know how to make friends.

Ifwafwa

It is a long way to Kasama to visit Chitimukulu. Many hours on the bus which leaves in the dark of the morning and arrives in the dark of the night. A young man who I share an ancestor with drives the bus and he will let me travel for nothing if it is not full. I will sleep so my head is clear when I see Chitimukulu.

Chitimukulu knows me from the time I cleared the snakes before the Ukusefya Pa Ng'wena ceremony, the one where we remember our journey from the Kola kingdom. He is a good man and there is kindness in his eyes. But when his people do wrong against others, he is very stern. He stands tall like the great tree he is named after and there is no wind, good or bad, that could blow him over. I will put my trust in him and hope that the girl does not get impatient while she waits. She wants everything to happen as soon as the words are out of her mouth. It is because she is young. She needs to learn that it does not always happen that way. Not here in Zambia, not anywhere in the world. Here we think for a long time and then we do the right thing, not the fast thing.

Bul-Boo

In the bright light of the morning, talking to Fred's great-granny didn't seem like such a good idea. How would you start a conversation like that with a renowned witch? And anyway, what was I going to ask her to do? I remember reading somewhere that if you ask for intervention from a witch, you have to ask for something specific otherwise you leave her with too many choices. A witch with choices, they say, is not a good thing.

I spoke to Fred about it, and you'd have to know Fred to understand his response. He believes in so many things that he finds it hard to keep track of them all. He believes, for example, that if you turn around twice in front of a door, good things will happen to you when you open it. Or that if you put the tea in your mug before the milk, the milk will sulk and that's when it curdles. Or that your bed has to face the sunrise otherwise you might not wake up at all. And thousands of things like that. He lives his life by little rules, most of which make no sense.

So at breaktime I told Fred I had to talk to him and we went down to the bottom of the playground to the fallen tree. No one else goes there because a girl in Grade Four once saw a snake there and ran screaming up to the gate. It's the best tree for sitting on because the trunk is so thick. Sister Leonisa says it was struck by lightning one afternoon after two girls in the school wrote rude things about her on the chalkboard. With the things she says, she is almost as bad as Madillo and Fred. When she told us that story, I asked her whether the two girls had been sitting under the tree when it was hit (just to see how far she would take it) and her answer was, "No, they weren't. But they might have been – and then they would have been sorry." Sister Leonisa may be a nun, but sometimes she has a strange attitude when it comes to things like hope and love.

"Fred, I'm thinking of asking your great-granny to solve this Winifred thing," I said.

He shook his head. "Bul-Boo, you'd better be very, very careful asking her. She's old now – perhaps the oldest person in Zambia – and while her powers are getting stronger and stronger every year, her memory isn't. She could just forget that it was you who asked her to put a curse on the old man and think instead that the old man asked her to put a spell on you. Then you could find yourself turned into a chameleon, and that wouldn't help Winifred at all."

"A *chameleon*? Why a chameleon?"

"That's her favourite creature, and she was saying the other day that there don't seem to be many around any more. She wants one for the garden, so she'd probably put you in a box and then bring you out now and again."

So suddenly I'm going to be a chameleon locked up in a box? And his great famous witch granny has a bad memory?

"I'm not listening any more. You told us she was the greatest, most powerful witch ever, but I don't believe she's even a witch – whatever a witch is when it's at home. You just made it all up. This is a stupid conversation anyway."

Fred looked at me and said, in his most solemn voice, "You should believe me, Bul-Boo. All I am saying is that her memory is not as good as it was and she gets confused. She's old. Dad says that even when he was small she was close to a hundred. Old people are entitled to lose their memories, even witches. You're a non-believer, anyway, so I don't think it's a good idea for you to ask her anything at all. She'll know you don't believe in her and then you'd be lucky to get away with becoming a chameleon – she might just decide to teach you a lesson and turn you into a dung-beetle. How about that? You'd spend the rest of your life rolling balls of dung around, then feasting on them."

That's the other thing about Fred: he finds himself very funny. While he was telling me this he was creeping about on the ground pretending to be a dung-beetle. Snuffling and slurping, which, as I told him, made him look more like a warthog. I knew I had lost him then. And even though I didn't believe anything he was saying, asking his great-granny for help was starting to look like even more of a bad idea.

When Fred had finished being a dung-beetle he started scratching in the dirt with a pen that had lost its ink and humming the Zambian national anthem. But he's still my favourite friend who's a boy, even if he makes up bad stories and pretends they are real.

Ifwafwa

The windows of the bus carry the soil of my land. I do not know the world beyond this red earth and the trees that spread their branches wide like umbrellas. I do not know the lands that my grandmother spoke of, the Kola kingdom to the south of us, the kingdom that ends at the sea. The pictures I have seen of the sea make my stomach feel empty. There is no end to the water, it carries on until there is nowhere to go. My grandmother told me that it ends in the middle of the earth, where the water is so black that nothing can be seen. That creatures live there who do not know the air. I do not want to go there if I cannot see the end of it.

I know the water inside Zambia, the lakes that are

quiet except when the rains come, the brown rivers that cover the crocodiles' heads. I know where you need to look for their eyes because the water can't hide those.

A woman sat next to me on the bus, she looked tired and her body seemed weak. She spoke to me of her first-born child, who is in prison for stealing. She was going to visit him. She told me she thought he would die there because he had the thin body of the prison disease. She had no food to take him and I had nothing to give her. Her face had already seen his death.

At Kasama I saw Chitimukulu. He has grown older and his walk has become slow, but his thoughts are not yet old. He told me that sometimes we have to do wrong to do right. That if something crosses our path and it is placing pain in the heart of a child, we must help that child. I will do that.

Winifred

My ma doesn't walk straight any more. Her back is bent and her eyes look at the floor. When she talks to me it's as if she doesn't want me to hear. It's because of what's happening, I know that. She doesn't know how to tell my uncle to take this thing away, to chase the old man out of the house. To send him back to the tavern so he can drink till he is dead. That is what I want: I want him to die so he can't look at me any more. I want him to disappear so I can be Winifred again. So I can go to school without feeling this big weight dragging behind me.

Bul-Boo says they'll help, but she does not know life like I know it. It all went wrong when Dad became sick. He died so slowly. Every day a little bit more of him went. I think it should be called the melting disease, because that's what happened to him: he melted like a candle, a bit each day until there was nothing left. When he got too weak to stand he would lie in the bed looking at you with eyes that were too big for his head. I could see all the bones in his body. I hadn't even known there were so many.

My mother told me that maybe he would get better, but I knew he wouldn't.

Then he was gone and my uncle came. He didn't come here when Dad was sick, but sometimes I saw him near the house. Waiting. He only came when there was death in our house and Ma was weak. He is loud and his voice is ugly. I know it's wrong to say, but I do not mind if they both die, him and his friend. There will be no hole left in this earth when they go. But there is a hole left in my body without my dad. I don't think it will ever be filled.

I know that I cannot be married unless my mother's brother permits it. But my mother has no brothers left now, she is alone. That is why my uncle thinks he can do this, he has no one to fear.

I wish I could wake up tomorrow morning and know that all this has gone away. I want to feel free to go to school and laugh and play with Bul-Boo and Madillo, or walk with them and Fred, listening to Madillo and her funny counting. I want to be free from these thoughts of this old man, but I can't. I want Sister Leonisa to look at me and ask me questions, but she doesn't any more – even though I am the only one who knows all the answers. Bul-Boo knows most of them and Madillo does too – except that the answers she gives sometimes are wrong in a funny kind of way. Like when Sister asked why Zambia was called a land-locked country. Madillo told her that it wasn't in fact landlocked because you could follow the Zambezi river all the way to the sea, and if you made a small boat out of tree bark and put it into the river, it would, one day, get to the sea. So that's not locked at all. Which is true. But there is no part of Zambia that touches the sea.

I wish that was all I had to think about right now.

Bul-Boo

As we walked past Fred's house on the way back from school today, I could feel someone watching us. There's a line of bushes at the end of his garden that is very thick. If someone stands behind them, it's hard to see who it is. (Unless it's Fred's dad, who is so big he could hardly hide anywhere.)

Madillo was way behind me, so I couldn't ask if she'd noticed, and as I couldn't see anything I just carried on walking. Then I heard my name: "Bul-Boo, Bul-Boo, Bul-Boo." A whispering voice. I looked and saw a very small hand waving through the bushes. It blended into the branches and looked as if it was growing. Only Fred's great-granny has a hand that small. Even his little brother, the one Madillo thinks is a hermaphrodite, has bigger hands than she does.

I felt a small lump of terror inside me as I remembered Fred's words. I was not ready to experience life as a dung-beetle. Not even as a chameleon, although I love them and their funny dinosaur ways. I love the way they change colour to suit where they are. I've always wanted to be able to do that, although not necessarily as a chameleon. The voice got louder. "Come here, little girl. It is me … Nokokulu … grandmother of Fred's father. I want to tell you something."

I find it hard to ignore anyone. If someone calls me, I have to answer them. Madillo doesn't seem to have that problem: in fact I think she likes ignoring people. But she wasn't there, so I stopped and approached the small hand. "Yes?" I said, hoping my voice would reach her as I didn't want to go too close.

"You are worried about your friend? The little girl with the smiling face?"

"Well … a bit worried."

"Bring her to me. I will fix everything," she said. Then the hand disappeared back into the bushes and it was as if it had never been there. I suppose she is so small that her footsteps aren't loud on the grass.

Now I don't know what to do. What do I say to Winifred, "Come and meet Fred's great-grandmother, an ancient witch with a bad memory, she'll sort everything out"? But if I don't tell her, the great-granny may get into a wild twitching rage and that's me done for.

Madillo had caught up with me by then and I found out the reason for the delay – she held out her hand and there, clutching her finger, was a tiny chameleon.

"It was trying to cross the road. I rescued it. I think we'll have to keep it, as it's too small to look after itself. I found the mother squashed."

I felt ill. Perfectly ill, as if I was about to fall over right then and there. It was like the time I fainted when we had to go to Mass at school. The church doors were shut and it was so hot I couldn't breathe. I remember looking at the priest and he seemed to get bigger and bigger, then the air around me went red. He loomed. The same thing had started to happen: the little chameleon grew and grew on Madillo's finger, so I closed my eyes and waited. I didn't faint, and once I had started breathing again I told Madillo to leave the chameleon on the hedge outside Fred's house because the great-granny was looking for chameleons and she would take it in. Sometimes Madillo can see when I'm not going to give in and she just does what I say. Not very often, but today it happened like that.

I wish I was back to my rational self: when I didn't believe in things I couldn't see. When I didn't start sacrificing small helpless chameleons on the altar of the great-granny. Life was easier then.

Ifwafwa

I will go to the girls tomorrow when I get back. I have a story for them that they will like. I hope they have not yet done anything about Winifred.

I know the boy who lives next to them, through Nokokulu. When I look at him I think he sees things in the same way as she does. She did not pass this on to her son or his son, the big one who makes a lot of noise. But I think the small boy has it. He does not know this yet and maybe he will never know it, but it is there – I can see it in the way his eyes watch me. I only met Nokokulu when I came to Lusaka, and it was then I learnt that she knows what will happen before it does; that she feels no fear. She knew me when she met me on the road for the first time and she called me by my birth name, Chishimba.

I was named for the falls near Kasama, for the guardian spirit that stays in the cave near the bottom of the falls. This cave is a place of peace and rest, a place without hatred or vengeance. I try to live up to my name, but there are times like now when I have to put it aside. The old woman reminds me of my name when she sees me. She is the only one in this new life of mine who knows it. To everyone else I am Ifwafwa or the Snake Man.

Bul-Boo

Ifwafwa came today. It seems so long since we told him about Winifred and I wanted to ask him many things. But if you ask him too many questions he closes his face up and you know he won't answer any of them. He told me once that if I am too impatient, my life will be ended before it has even started. Which is a slight exaggeration, as I have already had several years of my life, a little more than a start. I've learned not to be impatient with him by creating an imaginary wall in my brain. It is a stone wall that cuts off the question area. And it is very high, too high for questions to climb over. Today I had to put a roof on as well, otherwise I wouldn't have been able to help myself.

Ifwafwa mostly sits in the same place: just near the gate to our house, next to a large rock that Dad put there when we moved in. Dad liked the shape of it and Ifwafwa does too, because it warms his back when he sits against it. Sometimes, when the sun is very hot, he sits in the shade of the *muombo* tree that grows outside the garden. He told me that its red leaves, which arrive before the rains come, bring hope. Today his snake bag was empty.

"I have brought you no snakes today, but I have a story you will like," he said to Madillo. "It is the story of the Kariba Dam." Then he turned to me and tilted his head to one side. "And you, too, will like the story but you must be silent if you want to hear it."

As if I'm the noisy one!

"This is a sad story told by the BaTonga people who live up along the banks of the great Zambezi river. The river was home to Nyaminyami, which in English means "meat meat". Not a beautiful name for a river god, but a real name. He was a kind god who lived peacefully in the river with his beloved wife."

"What was her name?" asked Madillo, excluded from the keep quiet rule.

"What would you like to call her?" said Ifwafwa.

"Mahina, maybe? There is a Tonga-speaking girl in our class who told me that's the name of the moon. I like moons."

"A good name for her. So they lived in peace and harmony, troubling no one. When the rains were slow to arrive and the land was dry and thirsty, Nyaminyami would come slowly to the surface of the water and allow those who hungered to cut pieces of meat from his long, snake-like body. He was a creature of many forms: fish, snake and dragon, all in one body.

"One year, before any of you were born, Nyaminyami swam to one end of the Zambezi river and his wife, Mahina, swam to the other. They did not know what was about to happen, they were just enjoying a good slow swim. If they had known, they would have stayed together.

"Men came to the river with machines and they closed it off. They built a wall to stop its flow and they created a giant sea where before there had been nothing. The BaTonga people were forced to move from their homes, the animals ran away and the trees that had been there for thousands of years wept and died.

"Nyaminyami was angry that his wife was trapped many miles away. He stirred up the waters and the floods came. But when they died down, the men returned with even bigger machines and continued their work. Nyaminyami tried again and this time the wall broke and the machines were washed away. But the men did not give up.

"Meanwhile the BaTonga people were saddened because men had died in the floods. They begged Nyaminyami the river god to stop causing the floods, and he agreed. Which meant that he was never to see his wife again. Never to swim with her in the cool depths of the Zambezi, never to jump out of the water to greet the sun. Mahina had been the one who would heal Nyaminyami after he had fed the people, but she could do this no more. Without her he was lost, so he said farewell to the BaTonga people and disappeared silently, never again to show himself.

"But there are times when this great false sea shakes and shivers, when loud tremors come from the deep, when men hide in their homes for fear of the dark waters. That is Nyaminyami reminding them that he will always be alone without the bright light of Mahina to shine on him. He is letting the people know that he has not forgotten what they did. He is there, down among the drowned roots of the ancient trees. Remembering."

Ifwafwa sat back and closed his eyes, as he always does when he gets to the end of a story. Like I said before, I don't think he has ever told us one with a happy ending. Here we were left with an eternally sad creature lurking at the bottom of the Kariba Dam, its only thrill in life being to throw a few storms.

I then waited to see if Ifwafwa would mention

Winifred. He didn't. I decided I had to ask the question, otherwise I'd never sleep. "Ifwafwa … do you remember what we asked you about?"

He looked at me with disappointment in his eyes. "Little one, don't be asking me. I remember everything."

Which is not strictly true. He remembers more than most people but not everything. I didn't want to be the one to remind him of the day he left his bag of snakes behind. (Although there was some excuse because it was a very hot day and I know that if it's too hot my head gets foggy.)

"Ifwafwa," said Madillo, "one day you forgot the bag of—" I couldn't let her go any further, so I gave a loud yell. She got such a fright that she didn't finish her sentence and I was rewarded with a small smile from Ifwafwa as he picked up his bicycle and waved goodbye.

Ifwafwa

I went to the house today where young Winifred lives. I could not see her but her mother was there, sweeping the yard. Her back was bent low and there was no music in her. She is a young woman still, and strong – she does not look as if she has the disease yet. But it is a silent creeping disease, so it may have started its journey. She took no notice of me. It is mainly the children who notice me, they like the sound my bicycle makes. They like being afraid of the snakes when they know they cannot harm them.

I watched the mother for a long time. She looks like Winifred, but as with her daughter, the light has gone from her eyes. She swept and swept, even though there was nothing left to clean; the dust was quiet. When she went inside she closed the door. If she left it open, the small wind would make the house cooler.

I am scared of this thing I am going to do. My granny told me when I was very small that I should only use my gifts for good. It is hard to always do what is right, but I think this is right. The old man does not care about people and I know he would not listen if I tried to talk to him. He is a man who thinks great things about himself, a man who walks with his stomach before him, proud of all the beer that he fills it with each night. Proud to be a big man when all around him people are being emptied out by illness. Proud that he has a house with four brick walls and a roof. He needs that pride taken from him, and it is only the pale snake that can do this.

He is no good for this girl. He is no good for her mother, who is becoming old with the thought of him.

Bul-Boo

In many ways Madillo is some of the things I wish I could be. But in other ways she is not at all. I just hope I am not turning into her. I know that in some way, because we are identical twins, I am her and she is me, only not. I came out second, which is no bad thing: the Chinese say that the stronger one lets the weaker one out first. And I think that first bit of politeness has always stayed with me, sometimes I'm so polite that I don't let my real thoughts out.

Madillo doesn't have that problem. She thinks something and out it comes, *whoosh*. No matter what it is. I think a while before I speak, but usually I don't let the thoughts take over my brain. The thoughts are taking over now, though. Take, for example, Fred's great-granny, the witch. Here I am, terrified of being turned into a dung-beetle or a chameleon. (Mind you, dung-beetles were worshipped in Ancient Egypt, so their lives can't be all bad.) But, to be changed from me, a human being, into a dung-beetle? In the real world? That's what I mean: thoughts I should only be laughing at are taking over my mind.

I wrote in my notebook today: *Madillo is so free I wonder sometimes how she manages to stay on this earth. How does she not just float away? Not that I want her to, I just wonder about it.*

A long time has already passed since Winifred told me about her fate. And Ifwafwa thinks everything is going to be OK if he just says so. But it doesn't look that way to me.

The only solution is to let Winifred hide in our house until the old man gets bored or dies or finds another wife his own age. I think we could persuade Winifred to do that. The only issue would be Mum and Dad finding out. I decided to tell Madillo, because I couldn't do it on my own and I certainly couldn't hide Winifred from her as well as from Mum and Dad.

Before I could even get to telling her, she came out to me. I was thinking about the plan and I do my best thinking when I'm sitting on the step at the back door. It's very shady there and the step cools me down because it's polished and smooth.

Madillo knows she can always find me there.

"Bul-Boo, you remember I told you about my guardian spirit? Kasuba?"

"Of course I remember – you've told me about fifty times. And I hear you saying goodnight to him every night," I added.

"Well, perhaps *you* need one? If you had one, you'd go to sleep at night instead of lying awake then waking me up and dragging me downstairs with you. I think your head is too full of things: a guardian spirit would help."

"Help me stop thinking? No, thanks." If I stopped thinking, then what would I do?

"Well, why don't you just think about a guardian spirit and one may come to you?"

"Kasuba's little brother?" I said, sounding meaner than I meant to.

Madillo really loves this little spirit so much I almost believe he's real. She says I can't see him because I don't look hard enough. Apparently he's so small she holds him in the palm of her hand, and he has golden brown skin and a pointy nose. She says that he sits on the end of her bed and glows and that helps her get to sleep. Her own little spirit night-light. *Kasuba* means "sunlight", so I suppose that's why he glows. It is a nice thought, a little glowing thing sending you to sleep.

She'd gone quiet and I hate it when that happens.

"I didn't really mean that, Madillo. Sorry."

She just nodded, which made me feel worse. And so I never got to tell her my plan to hide Winifred. But thinking about it, I may as well tell her and Fred together tomorrow, because he'll find out from her anyway.

Fred's quite good at hiding things. One of the first things he told me when we first got to know him was that hiding things was one of his special talents. I suppose it's a handy talent to have, but I don't know what job it would get you. And since Winifred is not a thing, it may not be helpful at all.

We waited for Fred after school. By then Madillo had forgiven me for being horrible; it never takes her long to forgive. We don't often wait for Fred after school because he's one of those people who does everything: soccer, piano, drama and I don't know what else. Madillo and I don't do any of the after-school things because we like going home and having time with nothing in it. That's what's best about *after* school – that we get to leave school behind us.

Winifred is still not at school and I miss her so much. I have never been to her house so I don't even know how to speak to her about the plan. That means

I'll have to talk to Ifwafwa again and tell him her name and everything so that I can find out from him where she lives. I'll tell him I have to take her homework to her and hope he doesn't see through my lie.

Even though I'm sad that Winifred isn't at school, it was lucky she wasn't today because Sister Leonisa had one of her gory days. They seem to be becoming more and more frequent. We were doing geography, and this week we are on India. Sister Leonisa doesn't follow the book (I don't think she's even read the book), so each week she decides on a country and tells us everything she knows about it. Most times this has nothing to do with land or mountains or sea or trees or weather, or any of the normal geographical things. So for India we learnt about bride-burning.

She stood in front of the chalkboard, her hand clutching a piece of bright pink chalk, and began.

"Now, I want you all to listen very, very carefully today. In India, every one hour and forty minutes a bride burns to death. As I speak these words, it is possible that some poor woman is going up in flames. How do you think this happens?"

Although Sister always asks us questions, it's not because she wants answers. I have told Madillo that but she doesn't listen.

"Sister, do they spontaneously combust?" she asked.

"You know, when all of a sudden, with no matches in sight, a person just goes up in flames?"

"No, Madillo, that is not what happens. That doesn't happen anywhere except in comics. These women are burned by their husbands and their mothers-in-law, who are greedy for a bigger dowry. Do you know what a dowry is?"

No pause here. This time she made sure not to get an answer.

"It is a sum of money that the parents of a bride have to pay to the new husband's parents: a price for taking their daughter off their hands. Ridiculous! And not just money: they give them televisions, motorbikes, fridges, jewellery, animals… If the new mother-in-law doesn't think it's enough, she asks for more. And if no more comes – or if her son thinks a new wife would be a good idea anyway – they grab the bride in the kitchen, pour oil over her and light a match. *Poof!* there she goes. One young girl was set alight because the mother-in-law demanded a colour television instead of a black-and-white one. Can you imagine that? Burned to death because of a TV?"

Madillo interrupted. "But that doesn't happen all the time, Sister, otherwise there'd be no mothers-in-law left; they would have been burned too… In fact, there'd be no anyone because all the women would be gone, *whoosh!*"

Sister looked at her. "Did you hear me say 'all women' or 'all the time'? No? Then just listen, if you can. There are hundreds of millions of people in India: wonderful, beautiful, clever people. People who listen. But sometimes this thing happens. That's all I'm saying."

"Is that why you became a nun, Sister, so you wouldn't have a mother-in-law?" Fred asked.

I could see her actually thinking about this before she answered him.

"No. I became a nun because I thought it would be nice to teach young children. I was wrong, but it's too late to change now.

"It's not just the burning that goes on because of this dowry thing," she continued. "Parents who are very poor – and even those who aren't – don't want to have girl children because when the girls grow up the families will have to pay dowries. So they make sure they aren't born, and in India now there are more boys than girls. I think I would rather not be born than have oil poured over me and be burnt up."

That was Sister Leonisa getting all confused again about what she thinks and what she is supposed to think, being a nun and all that. And there aren't many people anyway who could tell her what to think, as she doesn't like being ordered about. I have learned a lot from her, although Mum says that some of the "facts" that come out of her mouth are dodgy. It's a good thing Mum didn't hear the tapeworm story.

"The lucky ones die when they're burned; the ones that survive live in agony for the rest of their lives and have to go back and be a slave to the old hag and her son who tried to kill them. If that was me I think I would burn *them* before they had a chance to try again. Or just run away – that might be the more Christian thing to do," Sister Leonisa said, turning her back to us to face the board.

The only time she uses chalk is when she does her wild drawings on the board. This one was of a stick figure running at high speed from a small house that had gone up in flames. I presume that this meant she had decided to take both options: burn the hag and her son and then run away.

I was thinking about it while we were waiting for Fred, and I know I'd run away before I had the chance to become anyone's bride.

I spoke to Fred and Madillo on the walk home. They both agreed with the plan to hide Winifred in our house, but Fred had one problem with it: the great-granny. I can't help it, but every time I hear about her it feels as though a battalion of ants is crawling up my back.

"If Winifred is that close, right next door, my great-granny will sense it. She will. She knows when things change. She knew my guinea pig had died before I did, and I was in the same room as it."

"That's not sensing something, that's murder," said Madillo.

Fred didn't seem put out by that. "No, I don't think so. He was upside down in his water bowl. If she had killed him, it would have been with a curse and he would have just been dead on the floor of the cage."

"Curses aren't always straightforward, that's ridiculous," said Madillo. "Most curses cause peculiar, horrible deaths. She could have said, "Guinea pig, guinea pig, in water you'll end. Guinea pig, guinea pig, you won't … mend?"

A ready-made curse? You'd think she had a store cupboard full of them.

"No," said Fred. "I had been trying to teach him to swim, so I think he was practising but forgot what he was supposed to do when he was halfway across. Anyway, all I'm saying is that she can see things from far away, so if she asks me I'll just say Winifred is visiting."

We didn't get as far as working out the actual plan, because we'd reached Fred's gate by then and I didn't want to wait around for the great-granny to appear. I wished Winifred was with us – she's the best one for making plans. But she wasn't.

We told Fred we'd work it out and then call on

him if we needed help. He might be a help because I think Winifred likes him. She gets a bit silly when he is around.

Ifwafwa

A gift that you have not earned is a precious thing. It is not to be played with or broken or ignored. I have tried to use my gift wisely in my life; I have not put it on show. I use it to help humans quieten their fears of these animals. To show that killing them is not always the answer. Snakes fear us even more than we fear them, but they will strike us if they need to.

I use this gift to take the snakes from the places that humans have decided to make their own and I return them to the places that we have left wild, where they can live in peace.

I think I may lose this gift if I use it against humans. But I must, because I cannot find another way. Time is running out. Yesterday I saw the uncle. He sat outside the house on a small box in the sunlight while the mother cooked. He has a voice that frightens even the cockroaches. He shouts at the woman when he wants something, and she brings him food with her head bowed low. He stole this woman from a dead man and now wants to give her child away. He is a man without truth in his body.

Winifred

I miss school but I can't go back there because some of them know what my life is to become. They know I'll soon be shut up in a house with this old man to see to his needs. I cannot do spelling tests now because there is no point. Bul-Boo and her sister are OK, they'll not look at me funny. I don't know what Fred thinks – he avoids my eyes when he speaks to me. Sister Leonisa knows and she has stopped asking me questions.

I'd thought I would be a teacher when I grew up. Not a mad one like her, but a teacher who'd make the children want to come to school. My desk would be tidy and I would teach them everything they needed to know in this life. The pupils would call me Miss Winifred. I'd dress like a teacher should dress and my classroom would be a quiet one. There would be pictures on the wall of all the different places in the world, all the different animals. I would see if Ifwafwa could come in and tell the children all about snakes. The people I taught would grow up to be anything they wanted to be: doctors, builders, nurses, pilots on Zambian Airways, anything at all. Maybe some of them would want to be teachers like me.

Now I won't do that. I won't do anything any more, only be a wife to an ugly old man. I don't want to become like my mother, scared to say anything: she doesn't even laugh any more. I don't want to sweep the yard all day long and cook food to fill his belly. I don't want my whole life to be like that. Perhaps my friends will help; they say they will, but I don't know what they can do.

Ma will not speak to me about this any more. If I try to talk to her when Uncle is out, she tells me not to worry, it will all be fine – I am big now. But I am not. I don't feel big enough for this. And I know that she doesn't believe what she is saying. I've heard her crying about it. I don't know why she's so scared. I never want to be that afraid of anybody. It's not too late for me to escape – if I had somewhere to escape to.

Bul-Boo

I like the idea of Winifred staying with us, but I don't think she'll come. She keeps things about herself very private. Even before all this we didn't know a lot about her. All we knew was what we saw in class: clever Winifred, tidy Winifred and smiley Winifred. We didn't even know that her dad had died until Sister Leonisa told the class. Winifred had been sitting at her desk like it was a normal day, answering questions and writing everything down as if it really mattered. Nothing would matter to me any more if Dad died. I wouldn't even come to school or talk to anyone, and I certainly wouldn't answer any stupid questions that Sister asked me. But Winifred has always pretended everything is

OK. Until now. Now she can't pretend.

I wish it had been something else, something like having to move house, or her mother having another baby with the awful uncle. But not this. I also wish I didn't know this thing, it makes me feel ill. If we bring Winifred to our house, at least no one will know where to look. Her mother will feel sad, but it's her mother's fault that this is happening.

If I ever have a child – and I don't think I will – I will never let her be given to an old man as his wife. There's no excuse for that. Mum would never let it happen to us. I think Winifred's mother is being weak and useless. Even to let the uncle come in and suddenly become her husband. Just like that. No going out, no asking, no nothing. Just a "here I am" and "I'm your new husband, whether you like it or not". Sickening. What's the matter with her?

Fred says I am too intolerant, but that's just Fred. He also thinks Madillo is. He can't give me any good reason why I should be tolerant, though. If you look up the word there are a whole lot of meanings for it, but one of them is "the capacity to endure hardship or pain". Which is all very well if you're a plant. But I'm not, and if someone does something that causes me pain or hardship, am I supposed to just be quiet and smile about it? I don't think so.

Take the martyrs, Sister Leonisa's favourite subject. From what she says, a lot of them could be described as having had a capacity to endure pain and hardship. In fact some of them seemed to enjoy it. She told us one story of a young girl who was martyred and had all sorts of perfectly gruesome things done to her and, to quote, "She kept a cheerful and joyful countenance throughout."

According to Wikipedia there were some people who quite literally looked for it. They went to the emperor and said, "We are Christians. Please kill us." Which he did, until he got bored or tired because there were so many of them. Then he told them, "Why don't you go to the cliffs and kill yourselves, if you're so keen?" He had a point.

What I don't understand is why, if all they were killing you for was believing in something different from them, they didn't just lie and say they didn't believe in it any more? If I was told I'd be killed unless I believed in a great god who had no eyebrows and was made of spinach, I'd say, "But of course I believe in him, he is the one and only." What's the harm in that?

Sister Leonisa said that she thinks our society is slowly rotting away because there are no longer people who will die for their faith. Then she did some of her drawings on the board to show the ways in which the martyrs were killed. Saint Sebastian was one of them. Every little part of his body had an arrow sticking out of it, and – so she tells us – the arrows didn't kill him. Because all her drawings are of stick people, you could hardly see which lines were arrows and which were Sebastian's arms or legs. Her follow-up drawing was of him being hit over the head with some kind of blunt instrument, which is what did kill him. And he was made a saint for that. That makes no sense to me.

Ifwafwa

When I was a small boy and had a pain in my stomach, my mother would take me to the bush with the healing leaves. She would place a small cloth around my eyes and lead me right up to the bush and I would eat slowly, leaf by leaf, until the pains were cured. As I stood there in the silence with my eyes blind to the world, my mother would pray to Lesa through our ancestors. My stomach pains always went away. The leaves are strong medicine, I know that, but it was Lesa who brought me comfort through the prayers of my mother.

I need his help now, but he does not interfere. He will not do anything to take this man away from the child. But he will know what I do and why I must do it.

He is my parent far away and will watch over me when I need him.

When I am finished with this task, I will go to my home place and find the bones of my mother and grandmother. Then I will bring them back to the earth in the proper way. In this world there are the dead and the living, and we are all one. The dead go into the earth to become part of what makes us live. That is what I want, to bring my mother and grandmother some peace and to clear my head of the bad memories. Then their spirits can join those of our ancestors and bring goodness to this life. I do not want to think of them wandering, lost, without a home.

Bul-Boo

I asked Sister Leonisa today if she had heard from Winifred; if she knew why she wasn't coming to school any more. All I got was a narrowing of her eyes and a strange high-pitched sound from her mouth, which I think meant either "No" or "Don't ask me". Sister Leonisa is one of those teachers who starts off the year by telling you that you can ask her anything at all, then when you do, she doesn't answer. I suppose it makes sense – she never said she would answer.

I shouldn't have made that my first question – I wanted to try and find out if she had Winifred's address, but I realized she'd never give it to me then. At break I asked Fred if he'd find out for me. Sister Leonisa likes him because he always puts on this really innocent face when he speaks to her, puppy-dog eyes all over the place.

"Sister, we've collected money to buy Winifred a little present," he said, "but we don't know where to take it. Would you be able to let us have her address?"

"What a lovely thought, Fred — there's a place in heaven waiting for you, dear boy. Of course I will. You come up here and I'll give it to you."

OK, so he got the address, but I don't know why she thinks that booking his place in heaven would make him happy. He's got years and years to go. Anyway, there it was in Sister Leonisa's neat handwriting: *Winifred, 10 B32/54 Alick Nkhata Road, Kalingalinga.*

That, I suppose, was the easy part.

But as I thought about it, I realized that if we were going to go to Kalingalinga to find Winifred, we'd have to tell Mum and Dad. There was no way round it. To get there we'd have to cross a field and then a road and then another field. And then find the actual road. Kalingalinga is not small. And there are so many houses there that it would be hard. It'd be OK if it was just number ten, but when you got to number ten you'd then have to look for a whole lot of other numbers.

We decided to tell Dad that we wanted to invite Winifred over on Saturday and then ask him if we could fetch her. He'd have to come, obviously, because he'd be driving, but that would be fine. He agreed. Saturday seems a long way away, but we still have time.

Madillo and I sleep in a bunk bed – no prizes for guessing who gets the top bunk. She tells me it's because of her numbers on the ceiling: she'd not be able to sleep if she didn't have the numbers up there. And there's Kasuba, of course, who apparently doesn't like the bottom bunk.

We have a cupboard in our room that's built into the wall. On the one side there is a big empty space for shoes. We don't wear shoes unless we have to, so that's why it's empty. (Well, we wear them for school, and if we have to go out we put on flip-flops – but those don't take up much room.)

So that's where I'm going to make the bed for Winifred: the shoe cupboard. It sounds horrible, making a bed in a cupboard, but she's quite small and I'm going to make it really comfortable with cushions and duvets. It will be warm, that's the only problem, but at night we can leave all the windows open as well as the cupboard door, and she should be fine. If I were her I don't think I'd mind where I slept as long as it was away from the old man. It's the best hiding place in our room, anyway, because even if Mum comes in she doesn't look in there. (Mainly because she says she cannot bear the sight. Winifred probably won't be able to bear the sight either, as she's so neat.)

I don't know if this is going to work, but if I wait for Ifwafwa we'll be too late. And the great-granny isn't an option because she's just plain scary.

Ifwafwa

I do not have much time left to prepare for this. I do not want to leave it until the last minute, as anything could go wrong. And they might decide to make the wedding earlier. I cannot take any chances with this thing.

Sometimes, when there's no time to think about things over and over again, it is better. When I was small I used to think too hard about everything until my head became sore. As if it was going to burst. My granny would take leaves from the banana tree and wrap them round my head to cool it down, then she would make me sit quietly out of the sun and tell me to think about the way that the trees grow. She said that my headache was caused by too many thoughts jamming hard against each other, and that if I thought about things that were very slow then I would feel better.

A tree grows so slowly that you cannot see it move, so I would think carefully about how each tree comes from a small seed and then about how many rainy seasons and dry seasons it would take for the tree to grow its branches and leaves and fruit. Then one small fruit would fall or one pod would burst and scatter its seeds and the tree-growing starts all over again. That kind of thinking would send me to sleep.

Now I don't have time for fast or slow thinking, all I have time for is doing. The time is coming soon, and I will be ready.

Bul-Boo

I saw Ifwafwa today but he didn't see me. Or I don't think he did. Maybe he's like Fred's great-granny. Madillo says she sees without seeing: sees through hedges and walls, across roads and rivers for miles and miles. Madillo has decided that that is the great-granny's special witch gift.

Madillo has a thing about gifts. She doesn't question whether there is such a thing, her only problem is deciding which one to choose. At breaktime today I was the one who had to listen to her theories because Winifred is not around. Normally it would be Winifred on the receiving end, or Fred, because both of them find it funny. Fred believes about half of it and Winifred normally pretends to but you can see her laughing underneath. Madillo doesn't always see her laughter, because when she's spinning a tale she doesn't notice anything apart from how amazing her own story is.

So today there I was wondering if we were going to have a maths test and Madillo was deciding whether she wanted a turning-people-into-things gift or a seeing-into-people's-heads gift.

"It's hard not to want the gift of turning people into other things," she said. "That'd be fun. You'd have to be careful, though – if, for example, I turned Sister Leonisa into a tapeworm, she'd need a host. And knowing her, she'd find me, wherever I was, and creep down my throat. I couldn't change her back once she was comfortably settled in my stomach, so I'd have to do the saucer-of-milk trick and I think I'd rather live with a tapeworm inside me than pull it out through my mouth." As she said this she opened her mouth wide by way of demonstration and I found myself imagining Sister Leonisa being changed back into herself while she was still inside Madillo. Gross.

"With the seeing gift, on the other hand, there's no downside that I can think of," said Madillo thoughtfully. "Except that it might turn out to be a bit much. If all the thoughts were floating around for you to look at, the air would be so crowded you'd probably forget a lot of them. And you wouldn't be able to think straight.

I find it hard to talk straight anyway, because my head is filled with more thoughts than I can actually say. It's not that there are so many of them, I suppose – it's just that they would sound funny to other people. So I keep them to myself. Are you like that, Bul-Boo?" she said, as if she had suddenly remembered that she wasn't the only one who could speak.

"I suppose so," I said, "but I think I keep even more of mine inside than you do. And I wouldn't like to see what people think but don't say. I wouldn't like anyone peering into my head, so I shouldn't be peering into theirs."

"Maybe," Madillo said. "I suppose it's different for Fred's great-granny. She was born that way – she can't help it. She didn't ask to be seeing things, so you can't call her nosy. I think I'll choose the turning-people-into-things gift. I just won't use it too often."

"As if you'll get any gift at all," I said. "Even if there was such a thing you'd be at the end of a long queue, and seeing as there isn't, it doesn't matter anyway."

"So you're saying Ifwafwa doesn't have a gift?" She knew I wouldn't have an answer for that.

The bell rang then, which made it easy not to answer. The difference between Madillo and me is that I wouldn't call what Ifwafwa has a *gift*, like some spooky thing. I think he just knows snakes much better than anyone else.

When I saw Ifwafwa, he didn't look like himself. He was pushing his bike, his snake bag was empty and he didn't notice anything or anyone around him. I wondered what was wrong. I didn't call him over because he would think I was going to ask him what he had done about Winifred (I wouldn't do that) and then he'd know that I'm impatient with him – which I am, it just seems as though time is passing by and nothing is happening.

We'll just stick with the cupboard plan. If he does something too then that's fine, but I can't depend on it, gift or no gift. It was horrible to see him looking so sad, though. It makes me feel bad for asking him to help us.

Bul-Boo

We had the day off school today for Zambian Independence Day. Dad said that when he was little they never got the day off. But the way he talks you would think he never got a day off school ever: that it was just 365 days' hard slog, no messing, no fun. Mum says he exaggerates everything. She says that when she met him he told her he came from Zambia, "the butterfly-shaped heart of Africa, a land of poets and princes". I don't think that's a particularly good example of him exaggerating, because Zambia *is* the butterfly-shaped heart of Africa, and the bit about poets and princes was just him trying to put it into words that Mum would understand. Because at that stage she knew nothing about Africa at all, so she wouldn't have understood if he had said it was a land of chiefs and tellers of tales and all sorts of wondrous things. Which it is. (But I agree that he exaggerates about what school was like.)

Anyway, Mum exaggerates too, so she can't talk. She was at a convent in Ireland and the way she tells it we are lucky to have Sister Leonisa, because at least she doesn't hit us or twist our ears or make us stand in dark corners until we "forsake the ways of the devil". Which is a relief.

Since we were all off for the day – Madillo, Fred and I – we decided to spend it at Fred's house. I only agreed because the great-granny was out. Fred said she'd gone to visit the graves of her ancestors and would not be back until late that night. I cannot imagine her going out, she looks too old to go anywhere. If I was her family, I'd be worried she'd just disappear, fall down a pothole or something. Her supposed witchly powers wouldn't do her much good then.

I found myself wondering the other night – when I had started thinking she might actually be a witch – that if she was, why had she let herself get so old and weak. Dad is her doctor and he often goes over there to give her medicines. I have never heard him say she's a witch. Surely a proper witch, if such a thing exists, would heal herself.

When we got to Fred's house, he said that because everyone was out, even his mother, he would take us into the great-granny's room – maybe we would find something we could use to help Winifred. Madillo was really excited and I agreed to go along with it because I wanted to see what the great-granny's room was like. It's not part of their house, it's a small house by itself round where the mango trees grow. Fred knows that she keeps her key under a stone near the back door. I asked him why she needed a key if she was a witch, but he just hushed me up. When Fred is in his own house he gets a lot bossier.

He opened the door and called us to follow. When we got inside we just stood and looked around us. The room was quite dark and Fred couldn't find a light switch, but we could make out a very tall bed in the corner.

"How does she even get into that?" I said. "Does she fly?" I giggled, which is not something I normally do. I laugh; Madillo giggles. But there I was, giggling.

"No, I don't," said a voice that definitely wasn't Fred's or Madillo's. Fred, by this stage, had found the light switch and I saw a familiar small head tucked up in the bed. I screamed. Madillo screamed. And Fred just ran out of the room.

I couldn't move; it was as if my feet were stuck to the ground.

"I don't fly. I don't even run or jump. But I do climb." I saw it then: a small ladder at the end of the bed.

I couldn't speak, and I turned to discover that Madillo had mysteriously abandoned me as well.

"What do you want, little girl, with your scared eyes? Come here so I can see you," she said.

I moved towards the bed – there was nothing else I could do.

When I got closer I could see her hands holding onto the sheet. They were like the claws of a bird we'd once rescued. It was a small bird with yellow on its wings – Dad said it was a weaver bird. When it started getting better, it used to grab hold of my finger with its feet and wouldn't let go. That was what her hands looked like. Thin and grabby.

"I'll tell you something, little girl. You have asked my friend, the one who knows snakes, for his help – for your friend who is young and clever. That's right?"

I nodded.

"My friend, the man who rides the bicycle, will help her. He is a good man. You must not make him rush. He needs time to think. Do not be impatient, it will not help her. Now go. And tell Fred I will move my spare key from under the rock because he must ask me when he wants to come here. I will say yes, but he must not go through doors that are not his to open." She lay back on her pillow and closed her eyes.

I walked out backwards, slowly, in case she changed her mind, then turned as I reached the door and dashed out, closing it behind me.

Fred and Madillo were waiting behind the bougainvillea creeper.

"I have a message for you, Fred," I said in my calm but irritated voice.

"Yes…?" he said.

"Do not go through doors that are not yours to open. Ever again. And the key to that door has gone, she will not leave it there for you to find. Do not bother looking for it; it will be far, far away. And if you do try to look for it, things will be hard for you." (OK, so the last bit was pure embellishment. Whenever Madillo is trying to explain something, Mum always says, "Madillo, if you left out the pure embellishment you'd be able to say what you wanted to say in one sentence." Which is true, but now it was my turn to embellish a little and I was enjoying it.)

"She said that? I don't believe it. I'm her favourite – she doesn't mind what I do. You're lying," Fred said.

"I'm not," I told him. "And the last thing she said was that you must never take anything for granted. You'll find that if you do, it will disappear before you know it. Maybe you *were* her favourite, but things change.

And Madillo, she had a message for you, too." Now that I'd started, it was hard to stop. It must have been the Madillo in me coming out.

Madillo actually looked scared. I almost felt sorry for her.

"She said that you shouldn't always believe everything that Fred says. Think for yourself. She also said that Ifwafwa will help Winifred and we must not worry—"

"I told you that, but you wouldn't listen!" Madillo said. "And I do think for myself."

"Fred, was it you who told your great-granny about Winifred?" I said.

"No."

"Then who did? Ifwafwa?"

"No, he doesn't come here because my mum is scared of snakes, so Dad has to kill them all. She is also scared of him – of Ifwafwa – because she says he lets the snakes out of his bag and then pretends he's found them in the house. She thinks his bag is full of the same snakes, all the time, and that they are tame and just do what he tells them to do."

"That's not true," I said. "But it doesn't matter. How does your great-granny know about us asking Ifwafwa?" I didn't really want an answer and I didn't get one, anyway, because Fred's mum and dad came back at that moment and I didn't want to wait around to hear what they had to say. Or rather what his *dad* had to say – because all we would get from the mum would be a silent scurrying past us.

Some Independence Day.

Ifwafwa

I saw small Winifred today. She sat inside the window of their house and watched everyone who passed by. She did not move. Only sat, holding her chin in her hand, waiting for nothing. I do not think she will run away, this one. She looks too tired, there is no hope left in her. I saw her mother again as well. In her face there is a memory of a smile, but I do not know if it will ever come back. Then I saw the uncle, the father's brother, with his friend. Laughing and showing their teeth. Off to the tavern to drink into the night, like every night, as if there is nothing better to do. I will be patient and wait for them. Not tonight, but tomorrow when the moon is beginning.

This is the time when the night shows itself only to those who know. For those who cannot see, the night will be dark and strange shapes will appear. Fear will eat away at their insides and their legs will go weak. That is a good time for me. I see everything, because the young moon is my friend.

Tomorrow night it will be so. Then I am done here.

Bul-Boo

Today feels different from most days. Most days, even during the rainy season, the first thing I hear when I wake up is the cicadas, who sing from the time the sun goes down until the early morning. The first thing I see is the sky and it is almost always blue: a Zambian blue. We once went on holiday to Ireland to visit our granny and grandad. The blue of the sky there is very different from here. It's as if someone has washed some of the colour out of it. It is a watery blue, which makes sense I suppose because of the rain. The sky also feels low in Ireland, more like a painted ceiling than a sky. Here the sky is big.

Today when I woke up, the sky wasn't blue and the

cicadas were quiet. The clouds had gathered very early, much earlier than they should. Normally they start gathering in the afternoon so that by four o'clock they're ready to burst. Then the rain comes down so hard that it stings you if you stand outside. (Which would not be a good idea anyway because the lightning would get you, and that is much worse than a sting.) Mum says she misses the gentle rain of Ireland because it is soft on your skin. I think I prefer rain that comes and goes. After a storm here you only have to wait a few minutes before going outside, because the sun arrives and begins to dry everything off, leaving it steamy and warm. I prefer that kind of rain to cold rain, however soft.

Today it's not going to be like that. It is a funny day and it feels heavy.

Ifwafwa

The name these girls have given me, Ifwafwa, is true in many ways. The puff adder is a slow snake, like me. It does not trouble anyone, or anything, unless it has to. It is happy to bake in the sun, on a rock or the road, or next to a river bed. But then, when it has to stir itself, it does. So quickly that it takes everything by surprise. And then nothing or nobody should be in its way.

I do not want to strike. I would be happy to be left alone so I could live my life in peace. But there are many people who do not want me left in peace. Mainly there is Winston, who has taken from me the ones that I love. Winston, with his cruel, small brain. Now there is this old man, who wants to disrupt the life of a child whose father has gone. I must stand in for the father as he sleeps in the ground. Maybe this way the mother will learn that the most important thing for her to do in this world is keep her child safe. She will learn to say no when a wrong is being done to her and her daughter. Maybe this way the mother will gain the strength to tell the uncle that what he is doing is wrong. He came for one night and stayed for a lifetime. It is not our way.

So, because of this, I must strike. I must call on the pale one, who will listen to me and do what I ask. When I have done that I can go back to my home village and hear from Winston where my mother and grandmother lie unburied. I will go there when this thing is finished. I am ready now.

Winifred

It feels as if the life is running out of me. As if I have no time left to be me, Winifred, myself. Ma told me that the old man wants this marriage thing to happen sooner, but that she said no. I'd thought she had forgotten how to; I'd thought she had lost her voice. Maybe she only says no to the small things, like whether something will happen sooner or later, not to the one thing I want her to say it to, the marriage itself.

Uncle is not like Father. He does not listen to her, he thinks she has nothing to say. His ears are closed and his mind is dull. I sometimes think he can't be Father's brother – I don't see how two children so different could come from the one mother. But he is. Ma's so different now, with him. From the beginning she got smaller around him, silent and sad. It is as if she grew older when Dad went. It's not right: she's giving me away as if I am a chicken or a goat. It's not that she's lost her voice, it's that she's lost her mind. I'll have to find a way to escape on my own, there's no use waiting for Bul-Boo or Madillo or even Fred. What can they do?

Tomorrow I'll leave. I will wait until the night time, until all the little ones have gone to bed and Ma is asleep. I will wait until Uncle has drunk so many beers that he cannot walk straight, then I will go. Maybe I'll go to Sister Leonisa at school and she'll take pity on me. Maybe she'll make me a nun, then I won't have to marry anyone. I don't really want to be a nun, but it would be better than this. Even if I had to listen to Sister's stories every day it would still be better than this.

The sky is so heavy today that people are moving slowly. The air has stopped moving and it feels as though the world has forgotten how to spin. Sister showed us her globe once. She plugged it into the wall and it lit up, a glowing earth. Then she spun it faster and faster, round and round. She said that if the earth started spinning a little bit faster each day, soon it would go so fast that we would all fly off into space. When we were in space we'd just float around until we eventually found our way to heaven. She says she wouldn't mind at all if it started spinning faster, because she's looking forward to going to heaven – and so should we be.

I'm not happy that the air is so still now. I wish today would be the day that the earth decided to start spinning at high speed, then I could fly off into space and never come down here again. Never see the old man with his dirty teeth. Never hear him and Uncle talking about me as if I'd had my ears sewn up and couldn't hear them. Never hear Mama crying to herself about this life which has made my father die and her unable to speak. Never again watch Sister Leonisa looking at me as if I am one of those lost souls she talks about, the ones who sit between heaven and hell for the whole of eternity. Never again be Winifred who must get married. I could just float until I felt like going up to heaven, and when I arrived, everything would be different.

Sister tells us that in heaven, if you want a sweet it just appears in front of your eyes. All you need to do is pluck it out of the air. Everyone in heaven is kind and no one shouts or says ugly words; no one goes hungry or thirsty; the roof does not have holes in it where the rain can come in. And everyone is the same. The most important thing is that no one dies in heaven, because they are all already dead. That way no one can leave you to try and be a grown-up person by yourself when you do not want to be.

I am going to go tomorrow, anyway, whatever happens. Maybe if I do, Ma will finally see that she can't be a half-person any more and she'll get rid of Uncle. And perhaps the world will start spinning faster and the old man will fall down and crack his head and that will be the end of him. I hope so.

Bul-Boo

I have prepared the cupboard for Winifred. It looks so comfy in there now, big soft pillows and cool sheets so she doesn't get too hot, and she can always come out of the cupboard once Mum and Dad have said goodnight. Then we'll shut our door, and as long as we're quiet it won't matter. Maybe once she's here I can ask Ifwafwa how much more time he needs. He'll probably say, "Don't worry, little one, time means nothing."

Which is all very well, except that in this case time *does* matter.

Madillo refused to help me get the room ready because she thinks Ifwafwa will solve this problem and it's wrong of me to have no faith in him. I asked her how she knows that for sure and she tapped the side of her head and said, "I just know." That's a great help.

If I could remember all the things Madillo "just knows", there would be no room in my brain for anything else. I asked her once to explain what she means by it, because it's not what I would mean if I said it. Her answer was even more frustrating: "There are some things that just come into my head and it is not for me to question who puts them there or what journey they took. All I need to know — and all you need to know — is that I am right."

I wonder where Ifwafwa is. I hope nothing has happened to him. He could have gone to seek help for Winifred and been run over or something. Although if that was the case I'm sure we would have heard: the great-granny would have told Fred, probably even before it happened.

I wrote about her in my notebook last night. Witches are mainly just people who get the blame. It has always been that way, because everyone wants to blame someone else for their sadness or misfortune. So I do not believe Fred's great-granny is a witch, just an ancient odd woman.

It felt a bit of a relief to write it down, because I had started to become really nervous of her and that's too Madillo-like for my own good. I have known Fred my whole life, and ever since he could talk he has made up stories. I don't know why I chose to believe this one. I hope he doesn't make things up to tell his strange little brother, Joseph. Joseph looks like he'd collapse into a heap if anyone said anything horrible to him. He definitely takes after his mother. Although I suppose he has grown up with the whole witch thing, sort of like a family tradition – "Joseph, pass the salt to Great-granny Witch, there's a good boy" – so maybe he's not as scared as he looks.

One of Fred's silliest lies was when he told us that the reason he could get through the hedge between our houses – and we couldn't – was that the bushes parted to let him through. This is one of the things he says his great-granny has passed onto him. I asked him to show me but he said that if anyone was watching him the bushes wouldn't do it. How convenient is that? Bushes that wait when they're being watched? They obviously don't part wide enough, either, because we always know when he's come through the hedge just by the look of him.

So all set now for tomorrow. Well, not really all set because I still have no idea how we'll get Winifred here. Dad said he wanted to take us to Munda Wanga Gardens, but that will just have to wait. I like going there, mainly because of the giant tortoises and the petrified wood. I love the fact that *petrified* really means "turned to stone" – because that's exactly how you feel when you're so scared you cannot breathe. It is just how I felt when I heard the great-granny's voice and just how I know Winifred will be feeling now.

Night Falls in Kalingalinga

The moon lay low in the sky and the soil was damp. There were few lights burning in Kalingalinga and people did not stir from their homes. There was something strange in the air, something heavy and unexplained.

In Winifred's home Mama was clearing away the food. Winifred had not eaten. She was still sitting at the window looking out at the silent emptiness of the streets. Uncle cleaned his plate and licked his lips. Across the table sat his friend, his chair pushed back so his stomach had room to breathe. He was angry that the young girl had not come to the table to serve him his food. He had heard her begging her mother, "Not tonight, Mama. Please, I don't want to be near him."

And the mother had let her off. A spoilt child.

But the food had been good and his stomach was full. Now he could go to the shebeen with his friend: the night was warm and cold beer would taste good. He didn't like being around this woman who was going to be his mother-in-law. He didn't like the way she looked at him. Her husband said she would do what he told her to, but there was something in her eyes that was not good. She was like the woman from his own village who ended up not marrying because she would never do what anyone told her. They called her Mukani, "the one who always refuses". This mother had the same look in her eyes, even though she pretended to obey her husband. The old man did not trust her.

He had already told his friend that when he was married he would not live near his mother-in-law – he didn't care for that part of the tradition. He had his own house in the village of his mother, and the young girl would come to live there – it was already decided. He would come back on weekends, when he was not working. That way he could have two lives, a town life and a village life. It would be good.

They set out from the house, these two men, laughing loudly at each other's jokes, their eyes already greedy for beer. They walked slowly through the streets, their noses filled with the smells of paraffin and cooking that crept out of the open doors of the small houses. They didn't notice that the streets were empty; that there were no children kicking balls, no children chasing bicycle wheels or pushing the little cars made from wire and Coke cans; no men sitting outside the doors breathing in the night air; no women calling the children to come inside before the mosquitoes got them. They did not notice because they had other things on their minds.

When they got to the tavern they did not see that there was only one other man there, a man they didn't know. They were too busy to notice a stranger in their midst. They were too busy through the evening to notice that he stayed there for the whole night, sitting quietly in the corner without even sipping from the tall brown bottle in front of him. He looked at them but they did not look at him. The man in the corner wasn't happy with what he saw; it gave him no pleasure to be sitting there hour after hour, waiting. But he waited, as he had a job to do. He would wait till dawn if that was how long it took.

The drinking and talking continued till late into the night. The barman was anxious to close up shop and go to the back to get some sleep. It had been a long day and night, and he was tired of these men. He knew them and didn't want to chase them away: they were good customers, even if they were tiring. He also knew the other man, the one who never drank from his bottle. He did not mind him being there.

The two drinking companions grew louder as the night went on, and it seemed that they had forgotten that the darkness should bring sleep. But as the sun started to shine its gentle light onto the horizon, the older man yawned and stretched his arms out. The other man nodded and they both stood up. Neither of them was steady on his feet but they helped one another and shouted their goodbyes.

The third man, who had been watching them all night long, got up and handed the full bottle back to the barman, thanking him for his patience. This was the man who, they said, would keep the snakes away from your shop without asking for payment; the man who said little but heard much. He had spent the whole night listening to the two men as they drank, but they did not know this. He could listen without moving his head.

He walked slowly into the pink light of the morning. He was without his bike, so many of those who were starting their day did not recognize him. He carried his bag over his shoulder and there was a slight movement in it. It could have been the cool breeze that heralded the end of the heavy, warm night. He kept his distance behind the uncle and the old man until they arrived at the quietest part of the street. Then he walked faster until he was only a few metres behind them.

He stopped and undid his bag. Slowly, a magnificent, pure-white snake slithered out. It lay at his feet then looked up at him. Ifwafwa bent down and whispered words to it. Then he stroked the snake, from its pale head all the way down its rippling body. Slowly and elegantly it began its journey, slithering down the road behind the two men.

The uncle could not say his words properly as he stumbled down the street, and each time he tried he laughed louder, clinging onto his friend's arm. They were both filled with the fire of hunger now, walking faster so they could get back to the house to find food.

The uncle stopped, out of breath – he had heard something. He turned his head and saw a pale flash on the ground behind him. He shook his head, it must be the beer confusing him. He walked on. Suddenly the dawn light changed and a brightness came over the two men. The uncle turned round. He saw the pale shape moving swiftly towards them. He saw it leap into the air and wrap its long body around his friend's neck. It stayed like that for only a second before it slid back down. The uncle stood there, his feet unable to move, as the creature turned its attention to him. Slowly, it moved up the side of his body and wrapped itself around his right arm. Then it was gone.

The soft dawn light returned and the uncle looked down at his friend, who lay crumpled on the ground, not moving. The uncle stared at his own arm where the creature had attacked him. His shirtsleeve was ripped off and a mark ran from his thumb to his shoulder, the mark of a snake. His arm burned and felt as if it was no longer part of him. He looked behind him at the empty street and saw a man crouching on his haunches, his hands held out in a welcoming gesture. Then he saw nothing more as his feet found speed and he ran, leaving his friend alone to face the rising sun.

Ifwafwa

It is done now. I can rest for a while and take my friend back to the place where he sleeps. He is not like other snakes, which sleep in the dry season and wake up when the rains come; this one sleeps for years and years, waking only to do what has to be done. He is never seen between those times. It is only I who know him. I was told of him by my grandmother, and it was she who passed down to me the way to call him. Today was the first time I have called on him to work. Now I have said farewell to him.

He works swiftly, like no other, and leaves a mark only when it is necessary to do so. With these men it was necessary.

The small girl, Winifred, will be free of him now and able to live her life. I hope that the mother will find her true self and make the uncle leave. It is time for that to happen. The work of the pale snake will strengthen her heart.

Dawn in Kalingalinga

Winifred's uncle ran down the street, moaning noises escaping from his mouth with each step he took. He could not bear to look down at the arm hanging at his side. He burst in through the thin metal door of the house shouting for help, and collapsed into the chair he had left not twelve hours earlier.

Winifred's mother was standing in the corner. Like a blind man, he had not seen her.

"What have you done?" she asked calmly She did not shout; she was used to him after too much beer, fighting and cursing, strutting into the house in search of bandages or food.

When he turned to her, she could see that this time

was different: his eyes were wild and filled with fear, his right arm hung by his side and there seemed to be a strange mark on it.

"Simon is lying in the street!" he shouted. "I don't think he can get up. It happened so fast I could not even see what it was. One minute he was laughing, the next he was gone, fallen to the ground… There was this light, a bright light, and then this thing…" He looked over his shoulder in terror, then back at his wife. "This thing attacked me, too. My arm… Look." He was sobbing now.

Winifred's mother came closer. From Uncle's thumb right up to his shoulder was a perfect drawing of a pale snake winding its way up his arm. On his shoulder was the wide-open mouth, its fangs dripping. It looked ghostly against his dark skin. She stepped back from him. "Who did this? Go and clean yourself up, this thing looks evil." She couldn't bring herself to touch it. "Simon is drunk, you are drunk. There's been no lightning this morning – look at the clear sky. What are you talking about, flashes of light?"

He sobbed louder. "I saw it, it was right there, this thing – this monster – it came to Simon so fast and then to me… This cannot be cleaned off, it's on me and in me, I can feel it move. It's waiting to kill me. Look at its teeth…" He started hitting his arm as if he was trying to kill the snake.

Winifred's mother moved back even further. "That's an evil mark. What did you do?"

"Nothing! I did nothing!" he cried. "There was this man in the street… I saw him calling the snake monster, it was white, bright, shining … it's his snake, maybe the one from the water? It's going to kill me; it's just waiting there to bite."

He pulled his head to one side to escape the thing on his shoulder while Winifred's mother looked on in fear. She heard footsteps and turned to see Winifred watching from the doorway.

"Ma," Winifred said quietly, "what's happened?"

"Your uncle was attacked – and his friend. He says it was by a snake, a white snake."

"There's no white snake that I know of, Ma. No such thing. Where's the other man?"

Her uncle tried to stand. "He's lying in the street… You must go and help him. The snake was around his neck, just like that, then gone…"

He sat down again, his legs unable to hold him any longer. "Maybe he's dead … maybe I'm dead… Get the doctor for me, quickly! This thing is moving, it's coming closer!"

Winifred looked at her mother. "Tell him to go, Ma. This thing is bad. Tell him, Ma: he must go now." She was feeling light-headed, as if the world had started speeding up – maybe this was its way of spinning the uncle away. "Tell him, Ma. You can tell him."

Her mother looked at her, her first-born daughter, so small and strong, standing there with her back straight; her child, begging her.

Then she looked back at the man who had come into her house after her husband's death, come in like a rude visitor. Like a hyena after a lion, grabbing at what was left. This man who was as loud as his brother was quiet. She hated this man who had made her weak.

Yes, she would do it. She looked at the brother of her husband, and for one moment it seemed as though the world had stopped: there was no one else here, only her and this man, sobbing as he pulled uselessly at his strangely marked arm.

"You," she said, "get out of the house! Get out and go back to your mother. You're not supposed to be here. You should never have come in your brother's place." She heard her own voice, but it was as if someone else was speaking, someone far away from this room, speaking from the bright dawn sky.

"Go back now to your mother; show her what you look like. Maybe she will help you wash away the moving snake. Leave me here with my child. We have no need of you or your friend – you can take him with you. We do not want him."

The uncle looked at her and he knew he would have to go. She wasn't shouting but her words were strong. He didn't need her to tell him; he was going away from this place where white snakes appeared from nowhere. If he was going to die, he would die among his people.

Winifred's mother turned and walked towards Winifred and they held each other close. Winifred felt all the fear leave her body as she watched her uncle get unsteadily to his feet.

He looked at both of them, terror in his eyes, and still holding his arm away from him he shuffled towards the door. It was a long way back to his mother's place, but that was where he would go. Maybe the people there would chase him away when they saw the pale snake on his arm, but his mother would not.

Winifred and her mother did not move, but as the door closed behind the uncle, Winifred felt her mother loosen her hold on her. Winifred led her to the chair and she sat down, breathing in and out heavily. They did not speak. Winifred went to the door and looked out. The uncle was walking strangely, as if one side of his body was heavier than the other. She watched as he made his way down the street, and in the distance she saw a bundle of a person lying absolutely still. As she watched she saw a slight stirring, a faint movement coming from the bundle. It was the old man. She knew she would never have to see him again.

She closed the door quickly and locked it, then went to the stove to light it for the start of the new day. It was going to be a good day. The old man would never come for her and her uncle was gone, he would never again shout in this house. The pale snake had silenced him. Now it was just her and her mother and the little ones. They would be safe and she would be Winifred, her own self.

Bul-Boo

It is funny how things work out. Well, not funny really, because people being hurt is never funny. Although some people laugh when they hear about death. Mum tells me that that's only because they're scared at the thought of their own death and think that by laughing they might terrify death so it will never visit them. This may be true, or it could just be one of Mum's theories. When she told me that, I wrote in my notebook: I promise only to laugh at things that are funny, not at things that are scary. Like death. I am very scared of death and don't like to hear about people dying.

We heard the news from Fred, who's always delighted

when he gets to be the bearer of important information. He came through the hedge (I was watching and can verify that it did not part to let him through) and told us in his most serious voice, "Winifred has been saved." As if he had done it, single-handedly.

"What do you mean?" asked Madillo.

"The old man is dead, struck to the ground by a pale snake that came from the sky in a flash of terror… He's dead and won't be anyone's husband any more – unless she, too, is dead, then they would be together for ever in dead unholiness…."

He trailed off at that point, because he had, as usual, got carried away with himself.

Dead unholiness?

"And Winifred?" cried Madillo in horror.

"He just said she's been saved, what's the matter with both of you?" I said, even though I knew the answer to that: gory imaginations, that's what. Fred was standing in front of us with his arms raised to the sky just to make sure we got the point about the snake coming from on high and I wasn't sure whether to believe anything he said.

"What really happened?" I asked him.

"Exactly what I said. The old man was killed by a snake that appeared from nowhere. And the snake was white. That's what my great-granny says, and she knows."

"Anyone who knows anything about snakes knows there's no such thing," I said. "A white snake would shrivel up and die in the sun. Give it half an hour and it would be dead. It certainly wouldn't go around killing anyone. I think she's making it up."

He shook his head. "You think what you want to think. I know what I know. The old man is dead and he wasn't even sick. He was just walking home early this morning with Winifred's uncle when this monster attacked him. Killed him stone dead in two seconds flat."

"Who found his body?" I asked.

"Well…" he said in a slightly smaller voice.

"Well what?" Here we go, I thought, the admission of a lie.

"Well, no one found his body… So it seems like he died, then disappeared into thin air. Just like that."

"Right. What did your great-granny say, exactly?"

"She said he's gone."

"If Madillo came to you and said, 'Bul-Boo has gone,' would you leap about the place telling everyone I was dead?"

"No," he said defensively. "That would be stupid. But there was this snake…"

"So what happened to the uncle, then?"

Fred stepped closer to me. "He's marked by the snake, all the way down his arm, like a tattoo. It won't clean off. And Winifred's mother has sent him away. He will not darken her doorway again."

I may not have mentioned this, but Fred's mother likes to watch old movies – she has a supply of them that she brought with her to Zambia many years ago. Fred watches them too and often sounds as if he's in one. But the fact that he was sticking to his story was making me think there might be something a little true about it. (Except for the death part. I could tell that was definitely made up.)

"You'll see," he said. "Winifred will be back at school tomorrow as if nothing's happened."

Fred wouldn't be saying that if he wasn't sure – if only because he wouldn't want to be proved wrong.

"And to think we did nothing," I said. "All our plans. What if she had been killed?"

Madillo, who had gone quiet for a while, started tugging at my shoulder.

"I told you Ifwafwa would sort everything out. You didn't believe him."

"Ifwafwa? Because of the snake?" I said.

She nodded.

I felt cold suddenly, as if I was back at the fridge door. Could Ifwafwa have set a deadly snake on the old man? Kind, clever Ifwafwa with his tales and his smile that made you feel that the sun would always shine?

Ifwafwa who would not even harm a snake? I didn't want to think about it at all. I couldn't believe he would do something like that. I just wanted Winifred to be OK, I didn't want to hear stories of awful things. If Winifred is back at school tomorrow acting as if nothing has happened, then that will mean nothing has. Except for the old man and the uncle going away for ever – that would be perfect.

Bul-Boo

Winifred was back at school this morning – just as Fred had said she would be – her uniform all neat and tidy, her hair braided tight and her smile big. It made me feel even worse to think that we had failed her. But at least she was back, next to me, and I was longing to feel that everything was all right again. Back to normal. Except I found it hard to feel that. I didn't want to think that the old man had died – no matter how awful he was. And if it was Ifwafwa who had something to do with it, as Madillo insists, that made it even more unbearable. I don't even like to think about a moth dying, or a locust or a dung-beetle – especially a dung-beetle. When Billy our dog died, it was sadder than anything.

When we heard about Winifred's dad dying, it was horrible. I think that maybe the old man got hurt but then walked away. If he'd died, then they would have found him. No one can just disappear into thin air like that, can they? I'm sure that's just Fred's story – and it's not a very good one.

Fred was wrong on this one, I know he was. Winifred wouldn't have looked so happy if the old man had died – no one would, because you would feel like it was your fault. She was happy because she didn't have to marry him and she could just be herself. (That's the best reason to be happy.) If I was her, I'd probably never marry anyone in my whole life after such an escape. I'm going to try and be normal about it; I'm not going to let Fred and Madillo bring it up ever again, even if I have to bribe them. I know Winifred won't talk about it, why would she?

One day I'll ask Ifwafwa about it, when there's no one else there. He'll tell me the truth.

As for Sister Leonisa, she behaved today as if Winifred had never left. As if none of this had ever happened. So did everyone else in the class, which isn't so bad because they didn't know anything. Except, that is, Fred, who looked at Winifred sideways as if she was about to explode. I'm going to speak to him about that – he's such a goon sometimes.

It's funny, because when I saw Sister Leonisa behaving like that, it was almost as though nothing *had* happened. As if I'd woken up after a dream I wished I'd never had.

But I don't think so.

In fact I know for sure, because of the story Sister Leonisa told us earlier today, which can't have been a coincidence. It all started because Madillo's shoes were dirty. Sister made her take them off and bring them up to her desk so everyone could see them.

"All of you, take a good look at these dirty, muddy, smelly shoes on my desk," she said. Which was very unfair, as they weren't smelly, they just had a bit of mud on them.

"Now, I want you all to close your eyes, keep the picture of the dirty shoes in your head and listen. There was once a girl who never cleaned her shoes. If the shoes had met a tin of polish walking towards them they would have said, 'What is this strange thing we see in front of us?'"

I was watching Madillo as the story unfolded and would have felt her anger even if I'd not seen her foot tapping. (Sister Leonisa told us in class once, "I happily jump in where angels and devils fear to tread." Never was this truer than now.)

"Each night, this girl – we will call her Mad the Bad – would place her dirty shoes carefully next to her bed, mud and all. Well, one night a puff adder wandered into her bedroom—"

"Snakes don't *wander*, Sister, that's just silly. Only things with feet or hooves can wander," Madillo muttered, just loud enough for Sister Leonisa to hear.

"Don't interrupt, please. *This* snake wandered. If I may carry on, this particular snake was pregnant, and very hungry, and she thought she smelt a rat. But it wasn't a rat, it was Mad the Bad's shoes. So the snake – we'll call her Puffy – sniffed around them a bit but they confused her: they smelt like the earth outside but they were inside this house. All of a sudden Puffy felt an urge to give birth to her babies. She would not normally do this on the smooth floor of a house, but here she was, desperate to pop them all out, and luckily there was the perfect spot for her, inside the muddy shoes. So, while Mad the Bad slept peacefully, Puffy calmly gave birth to thirty-five little puff adders."

Throughout this story Madillo herself had been huffing and puffing, but Sister had ignored her. Finally, unable to contain herself, Madillo blurted out, "Thirty-five? In one pair of shoes? It's just a lie."

"Madillo, keep quiet," Sister Leonisa snapped. "The shoes were big – they had stretched from never being cleaned."

Sister Leonisa stretches the truth beyond anything if

she wants to make a point. In fact, I'm not sure she even knows what the truth is.

"So," she continued, "poor little Mad the Bad woke up in the morning, and when she looked down at her shoes all she could see was a writhing, demented mass of puff adder. Nothing else. She screamed at the top of her voice for her mother, who came running into the room and rescued her little girl. And I can tell you that from that day onwards Mad the Bad had the cleanest, shiniest shoes in the school. Never again would her shoes become the puff adder labour ward."

Sister Leonisa turned to look at Madillo. "Perhaps, young lady, you will think twice before you come into my classroom with muddy shoes again."

Madillo looked up at her and her foot stopped tapping. "I'll do that, Sister, then I'll think three times and maybe four. I might just carry on thinking about it right outside the classroom door. Anyway, I like puff adders, so I wouldn't mind helping one out in her hour of need."

The room went silent, but I heard Winifred next to me trying hard not to laugh. Sister heard her too, and looked across at Winifred, and for the first time since I've known her I saw her give a little smile and a large wink.

It was then that I knew everything might just be all right.

Epilogue

The old man stirred. He felt as though a burning fire separated his head from his body. He sat up and tried to speak. No sound came out of his mouth except for a weak hissing noise. His heart beat faster as he stood up on legs that were shaking. He lifted his hand to his neck and face and felt smooth dry ridges all over them. He pulled his hands away in horror and looked around the street. It was empty apart from a man crouched down watching him. The man was still and silent and the old man recognized him from somewhere. He felt fearful of him and started walking slowly and stiffly down the road. He needed to get out of this town, away from here. Back home to where he would be safe.

The dawn light strengthened as he made his way towards the main road. At one house that he passed a small boy opened the door to bring out the crumbs for the chickens. He saw the old man and stared at him in terror, then ran back inside shouting for his mother. "Ma, I saw a devil man with a snake crawling up his neck and into his mouth. A white snake."

This young boy was known to make up stories, especially if he wanted to get out of jobs that had to be done.

"There's no such thing," his mother scolded. "Let me see."

She went to the door and looked outside at the retreating figure of a shuffling old man.

"Poor old man, to have a small boy making up stories about him. Get back inside to wash yourself for church. I don't want to hear anything more about it. A white snake? That's impossible."

Acknowledgements

Lots of thanks due...

To Tom, for everything. Without you this would not have progressed beyond a passing (and idle) thought. To Mum and Dad, for making sure we grew up happy, curious and with our minds open. To my girls, Amy, Christie and Kate, for inspiring me, reading and always believing in me, and to Aisling and Maurice for your encouragement and support. To John and Claire for reading and for banging the drum so enthusiastically. To Julia for first making me think, why not write? To my other readers, Bryony, Caroline, Eileen, Anne, Bryan, Mary, Pat, Sibh, Louie, Alice, Kiwi John, Becca, Ruth and Dieter, I hope you enjoy the finished product. And to Karen: Happy Reading.

More thanks...

To Sophie Hicks, a Wonder Woman among agents, and to Edina Imrik and the rest of the staff who make the Ed Victor Literary Agency such a good home for an author. To Siobhán Parkinson, teacher extraordinaire and inspiration. To Kate Thompson for knocking my beginning on its head and making me start over. To Gill Evans and Emma Lidbury at Walker Books for showing faith in my writing and for making this first publishing experience so good. And to Katie Everson for her beautiful design. To my writer's group, Crab Apples – Jean, Gemma, Una and Geoff – for friendship, support, criticism and entertainment! And to Amnesty for the work you do and for endorsing this story.

And finally...

Thanks to Zambia and its people. It is a beautiful country, and anyone reading this book who has not been there should put it on a list of places to visit. I wrote *The Butterfly Heart* for many reasons: one of them was that Zambia occupies a very special place in my memory and I feel privileged to have spent my childhood there; the second is that I once knew a young girl who was taken out of school and married off to an old man. I know now and I knew then that this stole away her childhood and her life. This should not happen to anyone, anywhere, ever. So this book is also for her.

Amnesty International

We all have human rights, no matter who we are or where we live.

In *The Butterfly Heart*, Winifred very nearly becomes a victim of forced marriage, while her mother endures what we call "violence against women". These are terrible abuses of our human rights, but they are not confined to fiction – the y happen to girls and women all over the world.

Human rights are what every human being needs to live a life that is fair and respected, free from ab use, fear and want, and free to express our own beliefs. Human rights belong to all of us, regardless of who we are or where we live. They are part of what makes us human. But they are not always respected.

Amnesty International works to protect our human r ights, all over the world. We are a movement of ordinar y people from across the world standing up for humanity and human r ights. Our purpose is to protect individuals wherever justice, fairness, freedom and truth are denied.

To find out more about human r ights and how to start one of our very active Amnesty youth groups, go to:

www.amnesty.org.uk/youth

**Amnesty International UK, The Human Rights Action Centre
17–25 New Inn Yard, London EC2A 3EA   020 7033 1596
student@amnesty.org.uk
www.amnesty.org.uk**

"Amnesty's greetings cards really helped me in pr ison. In total, I received more than 4,000 – amazing! I read each one: the best, I think, w ere those from children and other student activists… It amaz ed me to see that those children know about human r ights. What a good omen for the future!"

Ignatius Mahendra Kusuma Wardhana, an Indonesian student who was arrested at a peaceful demonstr ation in 2003 and spent two years, seven months and ten da ys behind bars, where he was beaten and threatened.